AWKWARD MAGIC

*Also available in the Target Adventure Series:*

TRAVELLING MAGIC—Elisabeth Beresford

*For other Target titles, see end pages of this book*

A TARGET ADVENTURE

# AWKWARD MAGIC

ELISABETH BERESFORD

*Illustrated by Judith Valpy*

*a division of*
Universal-Tandem Publishing Co., Ltd.
14 Gloucester Road, London SW7 4RD

First published in Great Britain by Rupert-Hart Davis, Ltd., 1964

First published in this edition by
Universal-Tandem Publishing Co., Ltd., 1973
Second impression 1974

ISBN 0 426 10153 7



Dedication:
*To Antonia—with love*

Printed in Great Britain by The Anchor Press Ltd.,
and bound by Wm. Brendon & Son Ltd., both of Tiptree, Essex

# *Contents*

## 1. *A Very Strange-looking Dog*

"FARES please. Any more fares?" shouted the bus conductor rattling up the stairs. But there was nobody on the top deck except Joe Dixon who was sitting on the front seat wearing his school cap back to front and a rather miserable expression.

"There's only me," said Joe, turning round. "And I've got my season ticket."

"Hallo, Joe," said the conductor, who knew him quite well. He came and sat down on the other front seat and put his feet up on the ledge in front of it, a thing Joe had always been strictly forbidden to do.

"Started your holidays, have you?" asked the conductor taking out a handkerchief and wiping his hot face.

"Yes, we've got six weeks," said Joe.

"It's all right for some people," the conductor said cheerfully. "I wish *I* got six weeks' holiday in the summer."

Joe said nothing, because he knew that was the kind of thing grown-up people were always saying.

"Have a good time then," said the conductor. He got up as the bus slowed down for the next stop and went rattling off back to the lower deck. Joe looked out of the window at the heads of the people who were bobbing up and down St James's Street. They all seemed to be having a wonderful time already. There were mothers carrying buckets and spades and picnic baskets, and fathers buying their children ice-cream cornets and long sticky pieces of rock with the word BRIGHTON stamped through the middle of them. But Joe's mother was dead and his father was in the Army serving abroad, so Joe had to live with Mrs Chatter who was very nice and a wonderful cook, but was not the sort of person who thought up exciting things to do in the holidays.

Joe knew that he was very lucky to live in a place like

Brighton, but he couldn't help wishing that he had a family, like the boys at school. Nearly all of them were going away for the holidays, and three of them were flying to France and had talked about it all the morning in loud, boastful voices instead of tidying up their desks as they should have done.

The bus jerked itself over the top of the hill and along the main road which grew emptier and narrower until it reached Kemp Town which is really the furthest end of Brighton, because after that the houses stop altogether and there's nothing but the rolling green Downs and the tall white cliffs until you come to the village of Rottingdean. Every time they went past a turning Joe could see the sparkling blue sea. He liked bathing, but it isn't much fun on your own, and those of his friends who weren't going away all lived at the other end of Brighton. Joe heaved a deep sigh.

"Royal Hospital," shouted the conductor.

Joe climbed down the stairs.

"See you next term," the conductor shouted and rang the bell, and the bus roared and rattled away. Joe ran down the steep hill towards Mulliner Terrace which was where he lived with Mrs Chatter. All the houses faced north towards the Downs which meant that even on the hottest day their fronts were cold and shadowed while their back kitchens got very warm indeed.

Joe was just rounding the corner, banging his satchel against his legs, when he heard an odd whining noise and then a voice which said:

"Go on, get out of it."

Joe looked cautiously round the railings and saw two boys, much larger than himself, hanging over some basement steps.

"Give us that stone," said the second boy and threw it. There was a scuffling sound and then a yelp of pain.

Joe felt himself grow rather pale and he would very much have liked to have turned round and walked away. But on the other hand he couldn't really let the cat or dog, or whatever it was down in that basement, have stones thrown at it. Joe pushed his hand down into his pocket and his fingers closed round something cool and hard. It was the police whistle his father had given him last time he'd been home.

"Let's get him out of there," said the first boy.

"Mind he doesn't bite," said the second boy nervously, and threw another stone.

Without knowing quite how it happened Joe pulled out the whistle and blew on it very hard. Both boys jumped, and the smaller of the two said.

"It's the police; come on."

"*I* can't see them," said the first boy, but he didn't sound very brave, so Joe gave another blast on the whistle.

"I'm off, even if you're not," said the second boy, and he went running off down Mulliner Terrace, and a moment later his friend went after him. Joe waited till they were out of sight, and then walked over to the basement himself and peered down into the gloom.

Something moved softly in the shadows and then whimpered.

"I won't hurt you," Joe said.

There was silence for a moment, and then a dog edged out of the coal-hole where it had tried to take shelter. It was quite the strangest looking dog Joe had ever seen. It was covered in coal dust for one thing, but it was also a very odd shape. It had a nose shaped almost like a beak, a thick matted ruff of hair round its neck, a body that bulged, and a long, stringy tail.

"Golly," said Joe.

The dog shook itself and looked up at him. It had very cold green eyes that glinted in a way that made Joe feel extremely nervous. He said cautiously:

"Good dog. Come on, it's all right, they've gone away."

The dog seemed to make up its mind that Joe was speaking the truth, for it gave itself another shake and then padded up the steps, its long nails making a clicking sound. Joe stepped back hastily, but the dog, apart from growling softly in its throat, didn't come any closer. They stared at each other, and slowly a wonderful idea came into Joe's mind.

He would take the dog home. He had never had a pet of his own, and you could hardly call Mrs Chatter's fat, tabby cat, Tiger, any fun because all it wanted to do all day was to sleep on the kitchen window-sill.

Joe felt in his pocket again and found a piece of string. He held it out towards the dog who sniffed at it, but didn't seem to take offence. With fingers that trembled Joe tied the string round the animal's neck and then tried to pull it towards Number 13. The dog planted its feet far apart and growled.

"I'm not going to hurt you," Joe said again crossly.

It was getting late and he'd never be able to smuggle the dog indoors without Mrs Chatter seeing it if he didn't hurry up. The dog moved forward slowly and Joe dragged it to his own basement and down the steps.

"Be quiet," he whispered.

The dog seemed to understand, for it stopped grumbling and pressed itself tightly against Joe's legs. It was very cold to the touch.

"Is that you, Joe?" called Mrs Chatter from the kitchen.

"Yes," said Joe, standing quite still, half in and half out of the door.

"Well hurry up, dear, and wash your hands. Dinner's nearly ready."

"I won't be a tick," said Joe, and pushed the dog up the narrow stairs to the first-floor front room where his best friend Mr Serafin lived. Joe knocked quietly and then opened the door and looked inside.

Mr Serafin was sitting in front of the window with his feet up on a stool and his hands clasped over his stomach. He had a large blue and white handkerchief over his face, and as he breathed in and out the handkerchief went up and down.

"Mr Serafin," said Joe huskily, "could I ask a favour, please?"

Mr Serafin snorted and the handkerchief blew right off his face and onto his waistcoat. Mr Serafin was very fat and quite bald, and sometimes Joe tried to work out where his forehead ended and his real head began.

"Dinner?" said Mr Serafin hopefully, opening one eye and reaching for his spectacles.

"In a minute," said Joe. "I've got a dog and I wondered if you'd look after it for me. Just for a little while."

"Ah," said Mr Serafin, and opened his other eye and put on his spectacles. "I take it Mrs Chatter doesn't know about this?" he asked politely.

"That's right," agreed Joe, and pushed the dog into the room.

"God bless my soul," said Mr Serafin, and sat up so suddenly his stool toppled over. "Where in the world did you get *that*?"

"I found it," said Joe truthfully. "Will you?"

"Does it bite?" asked Mr Serafin, staring at the dog which chose that moment to yawn and show two rows of very sharp, pointed teeth.

"It hasn't yet," said Joe cautiously.

"All right," Mr Serafin said slowly. "I'll have it in here, but only if it stays over by the door."

"Sit, boy," said Joe, and the dog obligingly did so with a thump. "I'll get your dinner," gabbled Joe, and ran out of the room before Mr Serafin could change his mind.

The kitchen was so full of sunlight and steam that for a moment Joe couldn't see Mrs Chatter at all.

"There's a good boy," she said, suddenly appearing out of the mist with a tray. "Take that up to Mr Serafin for me, will you? And then come back quickly or everything'll be spoilt. It's Fried Fish and Treacle Pudding."

Joe went back again up the stairs as fast as he could and found Mr Serafin and the dog looking at each other in silence.

"Queer sort of animal," said Mr Serafin taking the tray gratefully. "I've never seen anything like it in all my born days. Talk about a mongrel . . ."

"Thank you," said Joe, "I'm sure he won't be any trouble," and he bolted down to the kitchen again.

"Oh Joe," said Mrs Chatter as she handed him his plate, "I think I've seen IT at last."

To anybody else this remark wouldn't have made any sense at all, but Joe, who knew Mrs Chatter very well indeed, understood at once what she meant, for it was the dream of Mrs Chatter's life to own a washing-machine. As she did not believe in something mysteriously called "The Higher Purchis" and she had very little money, both Mrs Chatter and Joe knew that she would never be able to buy a machine. However, they always politely ignored this fact, and Mrs Chatter often spent her spare afternoons going to washing-machine demonstrations in places like Simmonds—"The Store That Has Everything." Joe had gone with her once and the man in charge had said that his machine could do anything, so Joe had watched very carefully in the hope that the machine would suddenly answer him back. But of course it hadn't.

"What was it like?" Joe asked, through a mouthful of Fried Fish.

"Wonderful," said Mrs Chatter dreamily, and told him all about it. "There's going to be a demonstration this afternoon," she ended up. "I was thinking of going to watch. Would you like to come too, Joe?"

"No thank you," said Joe, finishing off his second helping of treacle pudding. "I've—um—got something else I want to do."

"You're sure?" said Mrs Chatter doubtfully. "I mean it is the first day of your holidays and I thought we might—go and have a Fancy Tea afterwards."

"Quite sure," Joe said firmly. He went up to get Mr Serafin's tray, and found him already dozing off again.

"Queerest creature I've ever seen," he said sleepily through the handkerchief. "Please give my compliments to the cook and tell her that pudding was something to dream about."

The dog looked at Joe with cold green eyes, but didn't move.

"I won't be long," Joe whispered to it and went off to help Mrs Chatter with the washing-up which was something he hated doing, but which he couldn't really avoid. It seemed to him that they would never get finished, and when Mrs Chatter asked him twice more if he was certain he wouldn't like to go to Simmonds with her he nearly dropped a plate in his anxiety.

At long last everything was tidy, and Mrs Chatter put on her best blue coat and the straw hat with the pink rose on it. Joe almost pushed her along the hall and out of the front door, and as soon as he heard her footsteps die away along the terrace he bounded upstairs to collect the dog.

"Take it away, do," said Mr Serafin through the handkerchief. "It makes me nervous. I can feel it looking at me all the time."

"Come along, boy," Joe said.

The dog got to its feet and shook itself, and then followed him out of the room, its claws clicking on the lino.

"You need a wash first," said Joe. All through dinner he had been half listening to Mrs Chatter and half trying to think up some way of persuading her to let him keep the dog. Perhaps if it looked a little less ugly she might take to it.

Joe opened the door into the bathroom and pushed the dog inside. It walked round peering at everything and growling softly.

"You're going to have a bath," Joe said nervously. "A nice bath. You'll like that."

The dog yawned rudely, and Joe hastily turned away and put in the plug and began to run the water. The dog heaved itself up heavily and watched with interest. Joe went to the cupboard and brought out the strong carbolic soap which Mrs Chatter made him use when he got tar on himself from the beach.

He tested the water with his hand, turned off the taps and picked up a scrubbing brush. He looked hopefully at the dog. The trouble was it was such a large animal. If it stood up on its hind legs it would probably be as tall as Joe.

"In you go," said Joe swallowing. "Nice bath."

He went over to the dog and tried to pick up its back

legs. The dog promptly put its front paws on the rim of the bath, growled, and looked over its shoulder at Joe in a very nasty way indeed.

"In you go," said Joe bravely, staggering slightly under the weight he was carrying. And then he got the biggest surprise of his life, for the dog opened its peculiar, beak-shaped mouth and said quite clearly and distinctly:

"I shall do nothing of the kind."

Joe's mouth fell open, and with a painful thump he sat down on the bathroom floor.

## 2. *Looking for Treasure*

"I BEG your pardon?" said Joe when he finally managed to get his breath back.

"So you should," the creature replied, stepping over him and sniffing at the soap. "Quite a sweet smelling unguent, but rather too strong for my tastes."

Joe put his head in his hands, closed his eyes and counted slowly up to ten. When he had finished he looked up, fully expecting to find himself in his bed, with Mrs Chatter standing in the doorway telling him it was time to get up for breakfast. What he did in fact see was a pair of green eyes which were rather too close to his own for comfort.

"Dogs," said Joe shakily, "don't talk."

"Not in your language perhaps," the creature said stiffly, "but then I am hardly a dog. *I* am a Gryphon, Griffon or Griffin. Pay your drachma and take your choice," it added absently.

"What's a Griffin?" whispered Joe, seizing on the one remark that had made sense to him so far.

"You're very ignorant, aren't you?" said the creature in exactly the same tone of voice that Joe's Geography master at school sometimes used. "A Griffin—I take it we are going to use that spelling?"

Joe nodded silently.

"Very well. A Griffin is a fabulous creature of the Ancient World. A world, I need hardly say, which was a great deal better than the one in which I now unfortunately find myself. We Griffins are by tradition the keepers of Treasure—gold, precious stones, that kind of thing. I wish you'd shut your mouth, boy. I have no desire to inspect your teeth."

Joe shut his mouth with a snap that made his jaws ache. The Griffin nodded graciously and began to pad round the bathroom.

"And what is *that*?" it asked, leaping heavily onto

the stool and prodding with its beak at a tin on the shelf.

"Mr Serafin's tooth powder," said Joe. "Look out, you'll have it over."

But even as he spoke the tin crashed to the floor and a white mist enveloped the room. The Griffin sneezed violently.

"Bless you," said Joe, going down on his hands and knees and trying to sweep up what powder he could with the bathmat.

"And blessings on your head too," said the Griffin, inspecting its bedraggled appearance rather sadly in the steamy little mirror. "From time to time Treasure goes astray you know. Kings bury it before going out to do battle, and they're such a suspicious lot they never think of telling anyone where the place is, so if they get killed the Treasure's as good as lost. Then there are Slave Uprisings, very messy usually, not to mention Geographical phenomena which——"

"Geographical what?" interrupted Joe, whose head was swimming.

"Volcanoes erupting, earthquakes, tidal waves. Surely you've heard of *them*?" the Griffin said crossly.

"Oh, I've heard of them," Joe agreed, almost equally crossly, "but we don't have them in Brighton. At least, not since I've lived here."

"Must be a very dull sort of place," the Griffin replied. "We always had something like that going on when I was young. My word you should have heard the fuss there was when Atlantis sank. It took us nearly two hundred years to get our Account Books sorted out over that little lot. We did it though, we found everything down to the smallest gold goblet. I got commended for that job." It swung its tail proudly.

"Our Geography master says Atlantis never existed," said Joe, who was still smarting from the Griffin's rudeness in calling Brighton a dull place.

"Then you can't help being on the ignorant side if your masters know so little," the Griffin said almost sweetly. Joe opened his mouth to argue and then decided against it.

"Do you think there's some Treasure here?" he asked instead, wondering if he would have to go out and dig in Mrs Chatter's small back garden which never grew anything but parsley and nasturtiums.

"Hardly," the Griffin replied. "But somewhere in the neighbourhood there is a little hoard which we can't trace. My task is to find it, value it and mark the location, and now if you *don't* mind I should like to clean up. Water's no good at all. Have you no sacred oils? No precious creams? I've had a very long journey and a reception which was most unworthy of my rank. And what's more," it added, "I've got a nasty feeling I shall start scratching in a moment."

"There's the Rosey-Pol," Joe said doubtfully. "Mrs Chatter uses it on the furniture and it doesn't smell bad at all."

"Fetch it," ordered the Griffin.

Joe scampered away and came back a few moments later with a tin of polish and a clean dishcloth. He started work rather gingerly, for now he had got over his astonishment he was a little afraid of the Griffin. That creature, however, seemed to have quite recovered from its bad temper, and as the dirt was rubbed away it began to growl softly in the back of its throat.

"That's better," it said when all the Rosey-Pol had been used up and the dishcloth had been turned a particularly nasty shade of grey. "Well, what do you think of me, boy?"

"Smashing," said Joe.

And indeed the creature did look quite handsome apart from its odd shape, for its coat had a lovely golden glow, and it was holding its head up proudly, and then to Joe's amazement the bulky part of its body suddenly stirred and fluttered, grew and spread until a pair of wings were revealed. It flapped them a couple of times and then soared across the bathroom and landed rather awkwardly on the window sill.

"Not enough space," it muttered. "Such a small dwelling. Now, boy," and it turned on the open-mouthed Joe, "*food.* What can you offer me?"

"I don't think there is anything," stuttered Joe, remembering the Fried Fish which he'd finished up for his dinner.

"Lead me to the cooking quarters," the Griffin said. "And look lively, I'm starving. I speak the language rather well, don't you think? I only took the short course of two years, but then I was always a remarkably quick learner."

It flapped back to the door and opened it with its beak.

"Do be quiet," implored Joe who was frightened that Mr Serafin might wake up and come to enquire what the noise was all about. The Griffin took no notice, but padded heavily downstairs to the kitchen.

Mrs Chatter's cat, Tiger, who was sitting on the window sill, opened one eye and then leapt to its feet, its body arching.

"Oh, it's you, is it?" said the Griffin. "I thought there was a cat about the place; I can always smell them out. Not a very handsome specimen, but vagabonds can't be choosers. Come here."

Tiger edged cautiously across the floor, and the Griffin put its sharp nose up against the cat's ear and whispered something. Tiger's fur lay down slowly and he mewed. The Griffin turned back towards Joe.

"He tells me there's a humble form of slaughter-house down the street," the Griffin said. "I shan't be long, and on my return we will begin the search."

"Search?" said Joe.

"For the Treasure, simpleton," the Griffin said, and followed Tiger out of the open window and across the little patch of garden. Both animals disappeared over the next-door fence. Joe shook his head, and after burying the empty Rosey-Pol tin in the bottom of the dustbin, he tried not very successfully to wash out the dishcloth. By the time he had finished the Griffin had returned, licking its lips.

"Not a bad meal," it said. "Come, let us get started."

"Now look here," said Joe who had been thinking things over carefully. "First, we don't even know where to start looking for your Treasure, and second, I don't think I can afford to keep you."

"Afford? What is afford?"

"I've only got three and fourpence," Joe said baldly, "and I should think it'll take all that to buy new tooth-powder for Mr Serafin and another tin of Rosey-Pol and then there's your food and . . ."

"Money needn't bother you," the Griffin said grandly. "But I see your point. However, I am a creature of infinite resource so I will deal with your problem first."

"How?" asked Joe, "I say—can you grant wishes?"

For one terrible moment he thought the Griffin was going to fly at him it looked so angry. The green eyes gleamed and its swishing tail only just missed hitting Mrs Chatter's best cut-glass flower vase.

"I keep forgetting," it said at last, "how little you know. Griffins don't go in for the riff-raff of Magic. Grant wishes indeed! That's the kind of work they put the first-year students through, so don't ever let me hear you say such a stupid thing again. Now do hurry up, I haven't got much time for my task. Only about six weeks by your way of reckoning."

"But where are we going?" asked Joe.

"To the houses of your rich merchants, of course."

"I don't think we've got any," Joe said doubtfully, wondering if the Griffin was referring to the man who came round with coal on the back of a lorry. He was the only merchant that Joe had ever heard of, and he didn't look in the least rich.

"I suppose there are *some* castles, mansions or large dwellings in this town?" the Griffin said tartly.

"The houses in Sussex Square and Lewis Crescent are pretty big," Joe said doubtfully. "But what will happen when you go outside? People will start staring and they might take you away and put you in a circus or something."

The Griffin took no notice of this objection, but opened the kitchen door and padded off down the hall. Joe followed it unhappily. He could foresee the most awful trouble ahead of him, and he really hated scenes of any sort.

"You'll soon learn, my boy," said the Griffin struggling to open the stiff catch on the front door, "that grown-up people never do notice what's right under their noses. If they don't understand something they either pretend it's not there, or they blame it on the weather or something. You'll see. Now open this door, there's a good chap."

Joe gave himself up for lost and did as he was asked. But to his great relief the Griffin seemed to have spoken the truth, for hardly anyone took any notice of them at all. One old lady did snap her fingers at it and say:

"There's a nice doggie then."

But the Griffin walked past with its head in the air, and the old lady went back to reading her book. It was very hot on the Front and the tar had begun to melt a little so that the Griffin was soon leaving a little trail of claw marks behind it.

"This is Lewis Crescent," said Joe in a low voice as

they came to the bottom of a very pleasant square with some gardens in the middle.

"It's worth a try," the Griffin said, and quickening its pace it crossed over the road and began to walk alongside the railings, peering into the shadowy basements. Its ears were cocked forward as though it was listening for something, and Joe said desperately:

"I *can't* just go in and ask somebody if they've got your Treasure. I just can't. They'd send for the police and——"

But he spoke to the empty air, for the Griffin had suddenly given a little growl of pleasure and darted forward. Before Joe could stop it, it was lumbering down the steps and with one turn of its beak it had opened the basement door and disappeared inside the house. Joe leant against the railings feeling quite sick, wondering if he ought to run away and pretend he'd never seen the Griffin in his life before. It seemed a cowardly thing to do, however, so he hung on with his heart thumping so loudly he could hear it.

Two old ladies walked past slowly, and one of them looked very hard at Joe so he tried to pretend he was just waiting for a friend and gazed out towards the shimmering sea. The old ladies whispered together and then moved on, and Joe let out a sigh of relief. It was odd to think that only three hours ago he'd been afraid that the holidays were going to be rather dull. Now, with the Griffin around, they might prove far too exciting.

"Psst," it was the Griffin. It came bounding up the steps with a paper bag in its mouth and an almost smug expression on its face. It dropped the bag at Joe's feet and wagged its long tail just like a real dog.

"What's that?" asked Joe.

"A little something for your trouble," the Griffin said grandly. "I'm not ungrateful for what you have done for me. Those should cover the cost of the white mist and my unguent. Now let us move on before any trouble starts."

"But we can't——" Joe began, when there was a banging on the window in the basement. Joe jumped and looked downwards into the gloom. A pale face swathed in pink and purple scarves was staring out at him. It looked both frightened and furious.

"You are *slow*," the Griffin said angrily, and picking up the paper bag it set off down Lewis Crescent towards the sea front at a fast trot. Joe glanced from it to the face at the window and took to his heels. He caught up with the Griffin just as it reached an empty shelter. It was slightly out of breath, but very pleased with itself.

"Now look here," said Joe. "Where have you been and what have you got?"

"I didn't bother to stop and enquire," the Griffin replied. "It's funny you know, people are just as careless now as they were two thousand years ago. A more inefficient Treasure Guard I've never met. Fancy leaving goods like that lying about."

"What goods?" whispered Joe, sitting down beside the Griffin. It carefully laid the paper bag on Joe's lap and then sat back with its head on one side.

"A few trifles," it said. "In payment for your gracious services. Go on, have a look-see."

With shaky fingers Joe opened the paper bag and tipped the contents out onto the wooden seat.

"Oh glory," he whispered.

He was staring at a jumbled collection of necklaces, rings and clips which shone brilliantly as the sun caught them.

"Not bad, eh?" said the Griffin proudly, its green eyes glittering. "Not bad at all for a *first* attempt!"

# 3. *Grace*

Mrs Chatter sometimes said she wished the ground would open and swallow her up. Joe had always wondered what she meant, but at that moment he understood perfectly. He pulled a dirty handkerchief out of his pocket and covered up the jewels.

"It's stealing," he said.

"Pooh," replied the Griffin, but it looked a little less sure of itself.

"And you've got to give these back," Joe went on.

"Now look here——" the Griffin was beginning huffily when there was a clatter of footsteps and a small girl raced round the side of the shelter and threw herself bodily at Joe. There was an undignified scramble, and a diamond ring shot off his lap and was neatly caught by the Griffin in its beak.

"Give them back, give them back," said the stranger in a kind of desperate wail. "They're mine."

"I don't know what you mean," said Joe, who'd got over his first fright when he saw that his attacker was at least an inch shorter than himself and not, as he had feared in the first panicky moment, a policeman.

"Oh yes you do," she said, bunching her hands into fists and advancing on Joe once more.

"You'll break your thumbs if you hit people like that," Joe said. "Girls never can box properly."

"Stop talking," she said, stamping her foot with rage, "and give me back my jewellery. I know you took it because I saw you, so there!"

Joe looked at the girl more closely and realised that although she was no longer wearing a purple turban she was without doubt the white face he'd seen at the basement window. Relief gave way to a nasty sinking sensation in his inside. He glanced over his shoulder, but there was no sign of any furious parents bearing down on them.

"Girls don't have rings and bracelets and things like that," said Joe, playing for time.

"I do," she said triumphantly. She looked from Joe to the Griffin and went rather pink in the face. "Because as it happens I'm very rich. I've got about a—a million pounds. Perhaps even two million; I haven't bothered to count it up lately."

This astonishing statement took Joe's breath away completely. He had never seen a millionaire before and he had always imagined that they were elderly gentlemen who drove about in big cars and not small girls in creased cotton frocks and sandals. Even the Griffin seemed to be impressed, for it dropped the ring carefully into Joe's trouser pocket and then padded round to have a closer look.

"Go away," said the girl, flapping her hands up and down.

"Don't *do* that," snapped the Griffin. "It's not polite."

The girl sat down very close to Joe who had prudently been tying up the jewels in his handkerchief.

"It talked," the girl whispered.

"It's a very clever dog," Joe said quickly. "You won't tell anyone, will you? I mean they might take it away from me."

"All right," she agreed. "Actually I had a budgerigar once and that said Grace quite plainly. At least it did to me."

"Grace?" said Joe, whose head was starting to go round in circles. "You mean before meals—like you have it at school?"

To his surprise the girl chuckled.

"It's my name silly," she said. "Grace—er—just Grace."

> "*Patience is a virtue, virtue is a grace,*
> "*Grace is a little girl with a dirty face.*

"And if you don't mind my saying so, that's a particularly apt description at the moment," said the Griffin.

"I can't help that," Grace said, rubbing at one dusty cheek with her arm and only making the smudge worse. "I say, you do talk beautifully."

The Griffin preened itself and tried to look modest.

"About those jewels," said Joe, who was starting to feel that they were getting away from the main problem. "Supposing, just supposing I did happen to have them and you got them all back safely, you wouldn't tell anyone, would you? I mean anyone like the police f'rinstance?"

Grace dug the heel of her sandal into the soft tar of the promenade while Joe held his breath.

"All right," she said slowly. "I won't tell."

"Thank you," said Joe getting quickly to his feet. "Thank you very much indeed. Come on, Dog," and he looked at the Griffin which ignored him.

"Are you a real burglar then?" asked Grace as the three of them crossed the Front and made their way back up Lewis Crescent.

"*I'm* not," said Joe, who had stopped feeling afraid and was now merely hot and cross.

"What a pity," said Grace surprisingly. "I've always

wanted to meet one. It's very dull being a millionaire, you know; you hardly ever meet interesting people."

Joe didn't reply because most of his mind didn't believe that Grace was rich at all. However, his doubts were very shaken when she insisted on inviting them into the house.

"All the servants have the afternoon off," she said, skipping down the basement steps and opening the door, "so do come in and have a look round."

Joe didn't want to at all, but as Grace had been very decent about not calling the police, he followed her down the steps. Once they were safely inside the basement he handed over the handkerchief and then Grace led the way up to the ground floor.

"Some people don't know the meaning of gratitude," the Griffin grumbled. "I go to all that trouble, and do I get any appreciation? No! Human nature doesn't seem to have changed one jot—you do say jot, don't you?—in the last two thousand years. If you ask me——"

"Nobody did," Joe said shortly.

The Griffin relapsed into a sulky silence, but this only lasted a few seconds for Grace had now thrown open the door to the sitting-room.

"Shades of Olympus," the Griffin said, rudely pushing past Joe. "This is more like it."

It was indeed, for it was quite the most wonderful room Joe had ever seen outside the Royal Pavilion. The walls were covered in silky blue paper and the chairs in red velvet. There were dozens of photographs in silver frames, and the carpet was so soft it was like walking on the sand when the tide has just gone out.

While Joe was staring at all this, Grace crossed her arms and smiled, and the Griffin ran round and round making little whimpering noises.

"You see," Grace said, "I *am* a millionaire. You didn't believe me, did you?"

"I'm sorry," Joe said humbly.

"That's all right," said Grace. "I'll just put my jewels away," and to Joe's further astonishment she walked over to the mantelpiece, stood on tiptoe and pushed aside a picture. There was a little door behind it and she turned the knob on this a couple of times and a tiny panel opened. The Griffin immediately bounded across and stood up on its hind legs, quivering.

"It's my safe," Grace said importantly. "I keep all my most valuable things in it. Do mind out, you silly dog, you're jogging my elbow."

"I'm not a dog," said the Griffin, "I'm a Griffin."

"Oh, are you?" Grace said calmly and shut the door and put the picture back into position. "I suppose that's why you're such a funny shape."

"I'm a particularly beautiful shape," the Griffin snapped back. It lowered its voice. "And if I were you—which thank goodness I'm not—I should be a great deal more careful about playing with things that don't belong to me. If we'd been real burglars instead of reliable Treasure Seekers, you'd have been in the stew."

"Soup," said Grace. "But how——"

"Is all the house like this?" asked Joe, who had missed the whispered conversation because he'd been bouncing on the enormous sofa.

"It's better," said Grace. "You should see the bedrooms. And the bathrooms."

She led them from room to room, and Joe had to admit that it was quite the most remarkable house he had ever seen. His respect for Grace grew every minute, and it wasn't until the silvery chimes of the grandfather clock in the hall floated up to them that he remembered that he'd got to get home for tea or Mrs Chatter would start worrying.

"I think you'd better go now," said Grace who had also been counting the chimes. She sounded a little nervous.

"Who lives up there?" asked the Griffin putting its two front paws on the bottom step of the stairs which led to the top floor.

"Only the housekeeper," said Grace quickly. "Now do hurry up, there's a good d—I mean Griffin."

She fairly bundled them down the rest of the stairs to the basement and out of the door.

"It's been so nice of you to call," said Grace, regaining some of her old manner, and she held out a small and dusty hand. Joe shook it, hoping that that was the right thing to do.

"And you really won't say anything about you-know-what?" he asked.

"Oh no, no, of course not," said Grace, not looking at the Griffin, and she shut the door in their faces.

"A lot of it was fake anyway," said the Griffin as he and Joe retraced their steps towards Mulliner Terrace which now seemed more ordinary and dull than ever, after the glories of Lewis Crescent.

"It looked real enough to me," Joe said, "and what's more, now we're alone, please don't go stealing things again. We'll get caught by the police and——"

"Who?" the Griffin asked with interest.

"The police. And locked up in prison."

"Oh, you mean the Civil Guard," the Griffin said and swung its tail, snarling softly at a poodle on the other side of the road. "I can deal with them, I promise you."

"Well I can't," said Joe. He remembered how he had first met the Griffin and couldn't resist adding nastily, "Anyway, you didn't seem to be managing very well this morning."

"That's quite a different bowl of fish," the Griffin said loftily. "Tell me, who is that small woman advancing towards us holding an umbrella like a weapon of war?"

"Glory, it's Mrs Chatter," said Joe.

"Shoo," said Mrs Chatter, shaking her brolly. "Joe, there's an enormous mongrel following you."

"Mrs Chatter, please don't," said Joe, grabbing her arm. "He's only a—a stray, and I've adopted him. Please let me keep him, please. He's quite tame, honestly."

Mrs Chatter looked from Joe's pleading, rather tired face to the Griffin which was doing its best to appear pathetic. Its ears went down and its tail drooped. Slowly it flattened itself onto the hot pavement and a faint smell of Rosey-Pol filled the air.

"You're sure?" Mrs Chatter said uncertainly.

"I think he must have been very badly treated by someone," said Joe, who knew Mrs Chatter's kind heart. Her expression changed.

"Poor doggie," she said, "who's a poor doggie then?"

The Griffin slid towards her snuffling softly. Mrs Chatter put out a cautious hand and patted its head. The Griffin rolled onto its back and waved its paws gently. Joe gulped and Mrs Chatter shook her head.

"Poor lambikins," she said.

Out of the corner of his eyes Joe saw the Griffin quiver slightly.

"All right, Joe," said Mrs Chatter. "You can keep him tonight, but the first thing tomorrow morning you take him down to the Police Station. Somebody might be heartbroken at losing their pet."

Joe thought it highly unlikely that anyone could ever feel like that about the Griffin, but wisely held his tongue. Mrs Chatter opened the front door and the three of them went inside. The Griffin was given a bowl of water which it lapped up thirstily, and then, over tea, Mrs Chatter told Joe about her afternoon.

"Oh, it was a lovely washing-machine," she said dreamily, staring at the kitchen wall as though she could still see it. "I wish you'd been there, Joe."

"So do I," said Joe with some feeling.

He was tired and he'd had a very busy afternoon, and what was more, with the Griffin around he could see a lot more trouble looming up on the horizon.

"And what did you do?" Mrs Chatter asked, pouring out her third cup of tea and putting three lumps of sugar in it.

"Oh just walked about," Joe said vaguely.

"And what else *could* I say?" he asked the Griffin some

three hours later when both of them were going to bed.

"Don't ask me," the Griffin said unhelpfully. "I only did my best to assist I'm sure. Poor lambikins indeed. How do you think I felt? Me, who's been used to being treated with awe!"

"Well at least I've met a real live millionaire," said Joe, scrambling into his pyjamas.

"It was quite a respectable mansion. I caught some very interesting cross currents, but fakes always confuse the scent," the Griffin said and stretched itself across the floor.

"I've never seen a sunken bath before," said Joe, propping his hands behind his head and looking up at the ceiling which had criss-cross lines on it where the plaster had split. Sometimes he pretended the cracks were rivers and he was exploring them in a boat.

"Pooh, that's nothing," said the Griffin, which was feeling very sleepy. "The Romans had those thousands of years ago. Much better ones too. Bigger. Now please don't talk any more, I have to think about tomorrow."

"Tomorrow?" said Joe, sitting bolt upright.

"After we have paid our duty call on the Civil Guards," the Griffin mumbled, "I shall, of course, continue my search for the Treasure. Now kindly close up."

"Shut up," corrected Joe.

The Griffin's only reply was a deep snore, and after a few minutes Joe decided that the best thing to do was to follow its example and go to sleep.

* * *

He woke up quite suddenly because a noise had startled him. The room was nearly in darkness although a little faint starlight was coming through the open window. Joe sat up in bed, and at the same time he heard the Griffin move too. The rumbling voice of Mr Serafin out in the passage reached them.

"Most extraordinary," he was saying, "I'm absolutely certain Mrs Chatter that I had some tooth powder left."

"Never mind," Mrs Chatter said soothingly. "I'll get you a drop of Vim from the kitchen. That'll bring them up nice and white, and tomorrow I'll get you some more Tootho-Brush."

The voices died away and two doors shut. Joe whispered softly:

"I'd forgotten all about that—and the Rosey-Pol."

"I hadn't," the Griffin replied. "Don't worry about it. I have the situation completely under control. Now go to sleep, do."

Joe settled back, and after a few minutes his steady breathing told the Griffin all it wanted to know. It got up quietly and padded across to Joe's trousers which were on the chair. It pushed its long beaky nose into the pocket and drew out something which glittered brightly. The Griffin dropped the object onto the rug and turned it over gently.

"Quite a pleasant little trinket," the Griffin said softly to itself, its green eyes shining. And putting the diamond ring between its claws it laid down its head and went to sleep.

# 4. *Diamonds Taste Nasty*

"WELL, I dunno, I'm sure," said the Police Sergeant. He leant over the top of his desk and looked down at the Griffin, "What breed would you say it was, sonny?"

"A mongrel," said Joe in a low voice. He was afraid

the Griffin might hear and take offence. It might even enter the conversation and then there would be Trouble.

"A what?" asked the Sergeant.

Joe decided to tell half the truth. He got up on tiptoe and beckoned to the policeman to come closer.

"A mongrel," he whispered, "but I don't want him to hear in case I hurt his feelings."

The Sergeant's face, which was red already, took on a deeper plum colour.

"I see," he said, and wrote something scratchily on a piece of paper. "Found him, did you, in Mulliner Terrace?"

"That's right," agreed Joe.

Oddly enough the Griffin hadn't said a word since it woke up that morning, and Joe was beginning to have an uneasy feeling that yesterday had never really happened and that the Griffin was in fact just a large and peculiar shaped dog.

The Sergeant wrote down some more details, told Joe that if the dog hadn't been claimed within three weeks he could keep it, but that it would have to have a dog licence, and was just going to say something more when the door banged open and two policemen backed into the room.

"It is disgraceful," said a deep and powerful voice. "Utterly disgraceful. I shall write to the papers about it."

A tall and very large lady swept into the room. She was quite old and her white hair was piled up high on top of her head.

She wore a pink hat made of feathers, a long pink coat and, in spite of the warm weather, several yards of fur, most of which was now slipping off her shoulders and trailing behind her. She carried a shopping basket, a handbag, a black cane with a silver top to it and a pair of spectacles which were attached to a long handle.

The Sergeant stood up and ran a finger round his collar. Joe watched, round-eyed. The Griffin slunk into a corner and obviously tried to pretend it wasn't there. The large lady pulled out her spectacles, which had become rather caught up with her pearl necklace, and advanced on the Sergeant.

"I have been robbed," she boomed, and jabbed at his middle coat button.

"Now, Madam," said the Sergeant feebly.

"Don't Madam me," said the large lady, and folded her arms. The moment she did this the shopping basket hit the handbag and tipped over. Two packets of breakfast cereal, a lettuce and several potatoes fell out and bounced across the floor. Joe chased after them, glad of the chance to do something because he was afraid he was going to burst out laughing. He returned them to the Booming Lady who bent down and patted his head gently.

"Thank you, dear boy," she said. "I'm glad to see someone has some manners," and she turned towards the two policemen who were still standing by the door with their mouths open. Her fur stole slid gracefully to the ground.

All three policemen immediately sprang forward in an attempt to reach it first, and Joe, who saw that this might go on all the morning, decided that it was a good time to escape. The Griffin also appeared to have the same idea, for it reached the doors several yards ahead of Joe and bolted out into the street with its head hanging down, looking for all the world as though somebody had just beaten it.

"A ring," boomed the lady's voice behind Joe, "a most valuable diamond ring is missing. It has great sentimental value, too."

"Now, Madam, that is Miss . . ." came the Sergeant's voice soothingly. "Are you sure it's been stolen? I mean there have been other occasions . . ."

"I trust you are not going to be tiresome and refer to that time when I mislaid some trumpery pendant . . ."

The lady's voice died away in the distance, and Joe leant against the nearest wall and tried to get his breath back properly. The Griffin whined and tried to nudge him to move on, and Joe, after making sure that there was nobody near them, said.

"What's the matter with you? Don't you feel well?"

The Griffin, in fact, looked most peculiar.

"I *can't* take you to a vet," Joe said. "He'd know you weren't a dog at once."

The Griffin growled deeply and butted its head against Joe's legs.

"Oh, all right," Joe said. "Sulk if you want to, though what I've done to make you so cross I *don't* know. I suppose we'd better get the shopping done."

He pulled out the list Mrs Chatter had written for him on the back of an envelope. Joe wasn't at all keen on this job because people were always pushing past him, and sometimes it seemed as though he must have become invisible for all the notice the shopkeepers took of him. However, it was at least a nice, ordinary sort of thing to have to do, and Joe had had quite enough of adventures for the time being.

"We'll go to the Super-Market," Joe said. The Griffin didn't reply, but continued to look rather sick. It kept close to Joe's heels, and when they reached the shop it walked very quietly and somehow managed to slip past the girl at the cash desk without her seeing. But perhaps that was because she was looking at a long purple glove which a man in a dark suit had just handed her.

"It was found under Savoury Pickles," he was saying. "Really, people *are* careless. It's a very expensive glove too, top quality leather. I suppose it'll be claimed. You'd better keep it by you, Miss Gunn."

The Griffin's beaky nose twitched slightly and a gleam came into its green eyes. Joe was too busy trying to find the place where the floor polish was kept to notice this. He filled up the wire basket with Mrs Chatter's shopping and then glanced round for the Griffin. It wasn't there.

"Griffin," said Joe in a low voice. "Griff—Griff!"

"And what's the matter with you, sonny?" said the man in the dark suit, suddenly peering at Joe over the top of a mountain of tins which were marked, SPECIAL BARGAIN OFFER!! 2d. OFF!!!

Joe remembered that dogs weren't allowed in and muttered:

"Nothing."

"Off you go then, sonny," said the man, who looked the sort of person who didn't like children. Joe went off hurriedly and lifted his basket up onto the counter by the cash desk. Miss Gunn took the things out one by one and said in a quick, sing-song voice.

"And – one-and-two – and – two-and-three – and–elevenpence – and – one-and-nine – and – one-ten-and-a-half. Seven and elevenpence ha'penny *if* you please."

Joe paid up and pushed all the things into the paper carrier Mrs Chatter had given him. There was still no sign of the Griffin, and he was beginning to feel very worried indeed when it suddenly skidded up behind him and hit him in the bend of the knees. Joe dropped the bag, and the Griffin, exactly like an ordinary dog, immediately lifted the scattered packets up with its teeth and put them back in the bag.

"No dogs, *if* you please," said the man in the dark suit coming towards them with his mouth pulled right down at the corners. Then, just as Joe was about to apologise, the man stopped looking cross and beamed instead.

"*Good* morning, Madam," he said, rubbing his hands together as if he were trying to wash them with invisible soap. Joe turned round, and there coming towards them was the Booming Lady.

"Not Madam," she said, waving her stick at the man who dodged back hurriedly, "Miss. I wish to purchase some sweet biscuits."

"Certainly, Ma–Miss," said the man, sounding rather like a sheep. "This way *if* you please."

"One moment!"

Her voice was so loud that everyone else in the Super-Market stopped talking.

"That," said the Booming Lady, "is MY glove."

She whacked the stick down on the counter, and as she did so something which glittered brightly bounced out of the purple glove. It was, oddly enough, a little wet and warm, but it was still undoubtedly a very beautiful diamond ring. Joe glanced at it and had a funny sort of feeling that he'd seen it before somewhere.

"Come on," whispered the Griffin, pulling at his shirt.

"Good gracious me," said the man in the dark suit. "Is that a *ring*?"

"Of course it's a ring," said the Booming Lady. "*My* ring. So that's where—tut-tut. It is most rewarding to know that there are *some* honest people left in the world. I shall put a pound in your Staff Box."

"How very gracious, Ma–Miss," said the man in the dark suit, washing his hands with invisible soap harder than ever. "We have always prided ourselves on the excellence of our staff, you know."

"If you don't shift yourself," said the Griffin in a furious whisper, "I'll bite you."

Joe hastily picked up his carrier bag and walked out into the street. He was still puzzled by what had happened, but he soon forgot about it in his delight that the Griffin seemed to have completely recovered. Bad-tempered it might be, but at least it was its old self. It opened and shut its mouth several times and ran its long tongue over its beaky nose.

"Ugh, diamonds. Nasty tasting things," it said.

"I beg your pardon?" said Joe.

"Never mind," the Griffin replied hastily. "Well now, I've paid my debts, overpaid as it turns out, and it's high time we got on with some work. The sands of time wait not even for Pharaoh, you know."

"I can't help that," said Joe, clutching the paper carrier more firmly. "I've got to get these things home."

"Then I shall search for my Treasure without your aid," the Griffin said loftily.

"Not for long you won't," Joe replied. "You'll be picked up as a stray dog and taken to the Police Station."

The Griffin swung its tail.

"In my young days," it said huffily, "we had a saying about all roads leading to Rome. Now they apparently go direct to the Civil Guard. However, *I* am not afraid. I am, as it happens, a particularly fearless Griffin, renowned throughout the Six Continents——"

"Don't you mean Five?" Joe interrupted.

"Six counting Atlantis, of course," the Griffin said severely. It drew itself up, curling its tail and putting out one paw in a stiff gesture. It really did look rather splendid.

"I shall go bravely forward along the lonely path of duty and——"

"If you've got any sense you'll go straight home," Joe said. "Here come those two boys who were after you yesterday."

He felt in his pocket for the police whistle, and then realized that the trick wouldn't work this time as the boys had seen him.

"And however dangerous the road or perilous the journey—*what* did you say?" the Griffin finished in quite a different tone. "Great Caesar's Ghost! Excuse *me.*"

It shot off down Mulliner Terrace away from the advancing boys.

"It's that ugly great hound," one of them shouted and drew a catapult out of his pocket.

"Don't, oh, don't," cried Joe, quite forgetting to be frightened himself.

"Get out of it, you," said the bigger boy, and gave Joe a push that sent him sprawling into the gutter. The other boy pulled back the elastic and a dried pea sang through the air. At the very same moment the front door of No. 13 opened and Mr Serafin started to descend the steps. The Griffin shot between his legs, and before Mr Serafin had recovered from that the dried pea caught him painfully on the back of his hand.

"Ruffians!" shouted Mr Serafin, "Dolts, Louts . . ."

"Renegade Slaves," prompted the Griffin, quite forgetting itself in the excitement of the moment.

"Renegade Slaves," roared Mr Serafin, and brandishing his stick he came down the steps more nimbly than he had done for years.

The two boys took to their heels down Mulliner Terrace, and Mr Serafin, panting and puffing, went over to Joe and helped him to his feet.

"My poor boy," he said, "are you all right?"

"Yes, thank you," said Joe, dusting himself down. Luckily Mr Serafin had forgotten about the mysterious voice which had prompted him from the front hall, and when Joe saw the Griffin again it was crouched up against Mrs Chatter in the kitchen.

"There, there," she said, stroking its golden coat gently. "Did the nasty boys chase you then? Never mind duckie."

The Griffin looked up at her with sorrowful green eyes, and Mrs Chatter clucked her tongue and told Joe to unpack the shopping.

"That's funny," she said, frowning, "you've got the right change and everything, but there's an extra tin of Rosey-Pol and Tootho-Brush. Perhaps it was Give-Away-And-Tuppence-Off-Day. How clever of you to get them, Joe, because we certainly needed them."

Joe was as puzzled as Mrs Chatter, because he hadn't remembered getting the tins, but he decided not to worry about it because he had quite enough to do with looking after the Griffin. That creature however, was strangely silent and when they were alone together in Joe's bedroom it said lightly:

"I've been thinking things over. Brain is what is called for in this job, not mere pavement-pounding, so I shall stay here and meditate over my problem."

"If you're worried about those boys . . ." Joe said.

"Boys? What boys?" the Griffin asked rearing itself up onto its hind legs. "If you think a couple of worthless lads have influenced me in any way, you are completely mistaken."

"Yes, yes, of course," said Joe smiling.

"And you can stop grinning," the Griffin snapped. "That is gratitude for you after all I've done this morning." It stopped suddenly, and then came as near to a smile as a Griffin can, and went on in a much softer voice.

"I need some books of reference. Books about this—er—place in which I find myself. Please get me some."

But all Joe could find was a stack of very old magazines and some cookery books. After lunch he went to see Mr Serafin who was staring thoughtfully out of the window instead of having his usual nap.

"Books on Brighton?" Mr Serafin said. "You *do* surprise me. I thought you preferred comics, Joe."

" Well, yes," Joe said, shifting his feet. "But this is a sort of holiday task, you see."

"Ah, yes, I do see," agreed Mr Serafin. "Well I can lend you my library tickets if that's any help."

Joe took them gratefully and then set off on foot for the middle of the town. It was odd being without the Griffin because he had become quite used to having it around, and every now and again he found himself saying something to the empty air which made the passers-by turn and look after him.

The Librarian seemed just as astonished as Mr Serafin at Joe's request, but when he realised that Joe wasn't trying to pull his leg he took him over to a rather gloomy corner and said:

"There you are, my boy, all these are about Brighton, so take your choice."

Joe stared at the shelves clutching his four tickets. All the books looked so dull and he had a nasty feeling that the Griffin would expect him to do some reading as well. He got out one or two and was slowly turning over the pages when a voice behind him said rather shyly:

"Hallo, Joe."

It was Grace.

# 5. *The Griffin Takes to the Air*

JOE and Grace walked along the Lower Promenade towards Kemp Town carrying four library books and licking ice lollies. Joe had had to pay for these as Grace had come out without any money.

"When you've got so much, you see," she said carelessly, "it really doesn't mean anything and you rather forget about it."

"It must be wonderful to be rich," said Joe, as a Volks Electric Railway car clanged past them full of passengers. "If my father had a lot of money he could leave the army and open up a shop in Brighton."

"If you had a lot of money you wouldn't need to have a shop, silly," said Grace, licking up a trickle of pink ice from the back of her hand.

"Nor we would," agreed Joe who hadn't thought of that before, then he added hastily, in case Grace thought he might be asking her to lend him some, "but you never know, perhaps the Griffin and me really will find a Buried Treasure one day."

"There's no such thing," Grace said flatly. Joe opened his mouth to argue, and then decided against it, so he finished off his lolly and pushed the stick into his pocket, because you never know when that sort of thing may come in useful.

"How is the Griffin?" asked Grace as they toiled up the steps to the Top Promenade by the Banjo Groyne.

"He's OK," said Joe.

"Why don't you show him on television?" Grace suggested, "I bet you could make no end of money that way."

"It wouldn't work. He only talks when he feels like it," Joe replied quickly, "and he won't do it in front of grown-ups at all. Would you like to come back to tea?"

Grace said she would, and Joe took her along to

Mrs Chatter who, as luck would have it, had just made a whole batch of lemon-icing cakes.

"This is Grace," said Joe. "She lives in Lewis Crescent and she's a friend of mine."

"How do you do, Grace?" said Mrs Chatter, smiling, "Grace—er?"

"Just Grace," said Grace.

"I see," said Mrs Chatter politely. She seemed to take it for granted that Grace would stay to tea, and when the meal was over Joe took her upstairs to talk to the Griffin which was stretched out on the floor with one of the reference books on the floor between its paws.

"Never read so much nonsense in my life," it grumbled. "Half the facts aren't there and the other half aren't true."

"How do you know?" Grace asked, sitting on the bed and swinging her legs.

"Because I do," the Griffin said tartly. "As it happens I know quite a lot of things," and it stared at her very hard with its glittering green eyes. To Joe's astonishment Grace looked quite frightened.

"Have you found anything interesting yet?' Joe asked quickly.

"Not much," the Griffin replied. "There's a lot of digging to be done yet." It chuckled to itself and delicately turned the page with one claw.

Joe never did discover whether the Griffin was telling the truth or whether it was still scared of meeting the two boys again, but for several days it flatly refused to leave the house by the front door and got all its exercise by way of the back gardens up and down Mulliner Terrace. Mrs Chatter seemed to have become quite fond of it, and she bought up a whole pile of Woof-Woof dog food.

The Griffin ate it bravely, but confided to Joe that any self-respecting animal would much rather have plain ordinary meat.

So Joe had time on his hands, but he wasn't bored in the least, for he and Grace went exploring together. They walked along to Black Rock when the tide was out and went looking for Treasures which might have been washed in by the sea. They climbed up onto the Downs behind Whitehawk and tried to find a skylark's nest, but those intelligent birds were far too clever for them, and once Mr Serafin gave them five shillings—Grace never could remember to carry any money about with her—and they went on the Pier and had a go at a whole row of slot machines. Grace won a notebook with hardly any pages in it and Joe got a handful of pink and green sweets full of liquorice. And all the time the Griffin went on reading stolidly until one night it slapped the last book shut, rubbed its eyes, and said thoughtfully:

"We'd better try the Museum."

"The what?" said Joe, who was sitting up in bed, with his fingers in his ears, reading a comic. The Griffin sometimes mumbled to itself as it worked, which was most distracting.

"The Museum," the Griffin repeated. "It's a very strange case. Everything clear and straightforward and then suddenly the Treasure just vanishes. I suppose they couldn't have made a mistake in the books *my* end?"

"Couldn't you tell me what the Treasure looks like?" asked Joe.

"Sorry, Official Secret," the Griffin replied. "These things are—or should be—very closely guarded you know."

"Hush-hush," agreed Joe, nodding his head.

"There's no need to be rude," the Griffin said angrily. "I'll hush when I want to and not——"

"Is everything all right, Joe?" asked Mrs Chatter, knocking on the door.

"Yes, thank you," said Joe hastily, and turned out the light.

The Griffin was offended and wouldn't talk any more, so that when Grace came round the next morning all Joe could tell her was that he had to go to the Museum.

"What for?" asked Grace, who had been looking forward to a day on the beach.

"Nobody asked you to come with us," said the Griffin. "Why don't you order your slaves to take you for a ride in your chariot?"

"Because I haven't got one," said Grace.

"He means a car," Joe translated. He had got used to understanding most of what the Griffin said by now.

"I haven't got one of those either," Grace began, and then seeing Joe's astonished look she said, "I prefer buses. Some people do you know. Let's go to your beastly old museum then."

So they went by bus—Joe paid the fares—and got off in Old Steine and walked past the Royal Pavilion which was gleaming white and gold in the sunshine, and into the Museum. A man in uniform came up to them while Joe was examining a very strange clock in the entrance hall. It showed not only the time, but the day, the date and the month as well, and had a neat little notice underneath saying it had been presented in 1874.

"No dogs," said the man, sniffing and looking at the Griffin which was sliding about a little on the polished stone floor.

"That lady's got a dog," said Joe, pointing to a stout woman who had just gone past with a puffing pekinese under one arm.

"She's carrying it," the man said. "S'all right if you carries them."

"Then we'll carry this one," said Joe. "You take the front end, Grace."

The Griffin did its best to be as light as possible, but even so it was very heavy and extremely awkward. The sniffing man walked behind them as they staggered up the stairs.

"Soon as you drops it," he said mournfully, "out you go."

Then a whole lot of small children came clattering past, and the man forgot all about Joe and Grace and went after them instead.

"In here," panted Joe, backing into a long room full of glass cases containing skeletons. They put the Griffin down on its feet and it padded round, looking more and more upset.

"What's the matter?" asked Joe, who was sharing the last of the pink and green sweets with Grace.

"How would you like to see your old friends in this state?" asked the Griffin crossly. "It gives me the creepers, it really does."

"Creeps," said Grace, but the Griffin ignored her and went trotting off to the next room. There were no bones here, but a great many stuffed animals which were rather worse, for all their glass eyes seemed to be looking down with very sad expressions.

There were seals, snakes, monkeys, kangeroos, bears and dozens of other creatures, and round the walls were all kinds of birds. Above these were the heads of elephants, moose, deer and stags.

"They seem to be watching us," whispered Grace, who was keeping very close to Joe.

"Don't be silly," said Joe, who was staring up at the head of an American moose which looked as if it were just about to hiccup while the Sambur deer next to it appeared to be lost in thought.

"What's that?" asked Grace, stopping in front of a very queer looking furry animal which had a broad black beak.

"Don't you know an *Ornithorhynchus Anatinus* when you see it?" asked the Griffin in surprise.

"A *what?*"

"Duckbill or Platypus," said Joe, who had been reading the small notice under the animal.

"Strange creatures," said the Griffin, pushing Joe out of the way with its beaky nose. "Very shy. I remember once having a terrible time getting one of them to talk. It was during a Gold Rush in Australia; quite a lot of Treasure went astray then, one way and another."

"Did you find it?" Joe asked curiously.

"Naturally," the Griffin said in surprise. "I tell you what, there's one friend of mine they haven't got here, and that's the Unicorn. I *am* glad he got away. He was a great Heraldic Figure in his day, but he always had a nasty temper. There is a reference to this in the famous poem."

"Ah ha!" said a triumphant voice. "Caught you, haven't I? I knew you wouldn't be able to carry that dog of yours round for long."

It was the sniffing man. Joe made a dive for the Griffin and hauled it up into his arms, his legs bending like wet macaroni under the weight.

"Though I must say," the man said admiringly, "for a kid of your age you certainly knows a lot. It's marvellous what they teach in schools these days, it really is. Now then, off you hop."

It was more of a stagger than a hop, but Joe did his best to keep moving because he was afraid that the attendent might realize that it was the Griffin which had been talking so learnedly. Grace did what she could to help by holding up its back paws, and somehow they managed to get down the slippery steps, but in order to reach the street they had to walk past a big picture gallery and the moment the Griffin saw this it began to jerk about.

"Stop it," ordered Joe, his face smothered in the Griffin's rose-smelling coat.

"In there, in there," the Griffin replied, pushing and shoving against Joe's shoulder.

There were some chairs in the gallery so Joe stumbled

over to them and sat down gratefully. The attendant sniffed and moved on.

The plump lady with the pekinese was down at the other end of the large room, but apart from them it was empty.

"Tell me," said the Griffin. "Who's that?"

It pointed at an enormous portrait of a stout gentleman which was hung on the wall opposite. Grace ran across to have a look and came back to tell them it was a picture of the Prince Regent, later George the Fourth.

"He must have been a very *large* king," she said. "He's about nine feet high."

"They always had themselves painted like that," the Griffin said impatiently. "It made them look more important. If you could have seen the little squabs of Emperors I've met, you'd be surprised how different they were after the court artists had finished with them. Is the guard still about?"

"No," said Joe looking round.

"Here we go then," muttered the Griffin. It pushed itself off Joe's lap, ran a few steps and then launched itself into the air on its beautiful golden wings.

"Oh my," said Grace.

"Come back," ordered Joe.

But the Griffin took not the slightest notice and continued to swoop up and down in front of the picture like an enormous bat. The plump lady, who had been dozing happily, suddenly came to life as her little dog began to bark frantically.

"Yap, yap, yap, yap, yap, yap."

"Quiet, Too-Too. Quiet!" the lady said crossly.

"Yap, yap, yap, yap, yap, yap."

"I don't like it; I don't like it," said Grace, covering her face with her hands.

"Come down this minute, I say," commanded Joe.

The Griffin swooped past, making quite a breeze.

"A clue," it said. "A clue at last." It shot upwards again, its great golden wings just missing the picture.

"It's an eagle," shouted the plump lady, jumping to her feet and whirling her shopping basket round and round her head. "Help!"

There was the sound of running footsteps and the Griffin at last seemed to realise what it had done, for it wheeled round, glanced to the rear, and then swooped down the gallery straight for the plump lady. She gave a shriek which made Joe's neck prickle and then threw herself flat on the floor, while the pekinese very bravely jumped right off the ground with all four feet and tried to snap at the Griffin's tail as it shot past.

Joe shut his eyes and waited for the worst to happen. When he opened them again the attendant was running towards him with two more officials at his heels as well as a whole lot of ordinary people.

"What's going on here?" he demanded. "What have you been up to, eh?"

"Nothing," said Joe, who dared not turn round to see where the Griffin was in case it hadn't got its wings folded up yet.

"There was an eagle," said the plump lady who was being helped to her feet by several people. "It came right at me. It ought not to be allowed. I shall complain, I really shall."

"There, there, Madam," said the attendant, picking up her shopping basket and the pekinese which promptly tried to bite him. "We haven't got any live eagles here. You must have had a nasty dream."

"I did not," she said, stamping her foot with rage.

"Did *you* see any eagle?" the attendant asked Joe.

"No," said Joe truthfully.

"Nor me," said Grace.

"I tell you I *saw* it," said the plump lady.

"Then where is it now?" asked the attendant.

They all turned round and looked up and down the gallery. There were quite a few people standing at one end, but there was no sign of the Griffin.

Joe blinked and then noticed the old fashioned yellow and black coach which was on display at the far end. It was quivering very slightly as though something heavy had just moved inside it.

"I demand that you search this place," said the plump lady in a high voice. "I absolutely *demand* it!"

Joe crossed his fingers behind his back.

# 6. *The Understanding Wilkins*

THE three men went off down the gallery, with the plump lady keeping very close to them as though afraid that the Griffin might suddenly appear out of thin air and swoop down on her again. Joe stood quite still and held his breath. Now that all the fuss seemed to be over, the people who had come to watch the fun drifted away.

The attendant and his two friends were talking in low voices, and Joe felt rather sorry for the plump lady because he could see that they didn't believe a word she had said. They walked right past the coach, which had stopped shaking, and then came back to where Joe was standing.

"You're sure you didn't see no eagle?" asked the attendant, sniffing hard.

"Quite sure," said Joe, hoarsely.

"You see, Madam," said the man turning back to the plump lady, "a nasty dream, that's what it was. Why don't you go and have a nice cup of tea, eh?"

"Don't think I shall let the matter rest here," she said, putting her hat straight, "because I shan't!"

She went off very quickly, with the tail of the pekinese sticking out from under her arm and waving up and down like a lovely cream-coloured flag, and she was as good as her word, for she wrote to the local paper about it, and they printed her letter with the title:

*Local Resident Sees Golden Eagle*

It made quite a stir, and the plump lady, who up till then hadn't had many friends, found she had become quite important and was always being asked out to tea. But she never, never went to the Museum again.

So really the Griffin did quite a lot of good, but neither it nor Joe ever realised it. They escaped with Grace as fast as they could as soon as the coast was clear.

The Griffin smelt strongly of mothballs and complained that the coach had been a very tight fit indeed.

"Having to scramble about in that undignified fashion," it grumbled. "It's not my beaker of tea at all."

"There, there," said Grace soothingly. "But you did fly quite beautifully. I didn't know that those odd humps were——"

Joe nudged her hurriedly and she stopped speaking, but luckily the Griffin had only listened to the first part of her remark and was preening itself on the front seat of the bus.

"Oh, I don't know," it said modestly. "It wasn't anything *much* really, although I did pass out first in my flying class as it happens. Loops and whirls were my speciality."

"How splendid," said Joe, nudging Grace again because she was starting to giggle. "But did you really find a clue?"

"In a way," the Griffin said cautiously. "There's been so little to go on so far that I'm afraid I got rather carried away." It gave a hoarse coughing sound.

Grace patted it on the back, and the Griffin said sharply:

"That was a *joke*! Carried away . . . flying—see? Oh, never mind. Now do be quiet and let me do some thinking."

Joe was far too relieved to have escaped from the Museum to object to the Griffin's rather rude behaviour. He was also rather glad when the Griffin decided to stay indoors for the next few days to do some more reading.

Joe had had quite enough of hunting Treasure for the time being.

However, by the beginning of the following week the Griffin appeared to feel it had done enough work, and suggested a stroll in the town.

"Tell me," it said when they got out of the bus. "Where did that great and gracious Prince live?"

"What Prince?" asked Joe, whose mind had been on going for a swim.

"The Prince Regent?" suggested Grace. The Griffin nodded.

"Oh, him," said Joe. "In London, I suppose."

"No, he didn't," contradicted Grace. "Not all the time anyway. We learnt that at school."

"I'm glad to hear you learn something," said the Griffin. "I was beginning to have my doubts. Elucidate, O Fair One."

"I beg your——" said Grace.

"He means, tell him," said Joe, who could see what was coming and didn't like it.

"*Fair One*," said Grace. "I do like that. Although I'm not really fair a bit, except in the summer when my hair gets wet quite a lot when I've been bathing. Well, you know, the Prince Regent used to live part of the time in the Pavilion. That place there."

She waved towards the building they were just passing.

"A handsome Palace," said the Griffin approvingly. "Allow me to escort you inside."

"Escort whom you like; I'm not coming," said Joe, folding his arms and frowning. "We had enough trouble in the Museum. Goodness knows what would happen if you started to get carried away in the Pavilion."

"Oh, don't be such an old cowardy-custard," said Grace unfairly.

She and the Griffin went off, side by side, to a small door which had *Entrance* written up by it. Joe sat down on the grass opposite and sighed deeply. The Pavilion was certainly a very handsome and, indeed, most unusual building with its high white walls and huddles of little turrets which were all topped with domes—rather like enormous gold and white onions—but Joe was in no mood to appreciate it. He watched the pigeons instead as they pecked at the grass, arching their necks so that their feathers looked red and green at the same time.

Meanwhile, inside the Pavilion, Grace and the Griffin were meeting with an unexpected difficulty.

"I'm sorry," said the lady who sat behind a counter in the entrance hall selling guides and picture postcards, "but No Children Admitted unless with an adult, and certainly No Dogs."

"He's a very good dog," Grace said hopefully, and then, to the Griffin's horror, she added, "In fact, he isn't really a dog at all you know, he's a——"

The Griffin snarled loudly and looked so fierce that the lady behind the counter squeaked and even Grace backed away.

"Outside, *if* you please," said the lady in a high voice.

Grace knew she was beaten, so she turned round, and because she wasn't looking where she was going she walked straight into somebody who was just coming in. He was a tall, thin, not-quite-young man with a pale rather sad face.

"Whoops," he said, smiling, and then, when he saw Grace's disappointed expression he added more gently, "What's the matter?"

"I can't go in," said Grace. "Not on my own anyway. *She* won't let me," and Grace looked darkly at the lady behind the counter who was flapping a souvenir programme price 2s 6d at the Griffin which was inspecting the postcards.

"Dear me," said the man. "Well, well. And do you really want to go round the Pavilion?"

"Yes," said Grace firmly. Ten minutes ago she wouldn't have cared tuppence one way or the other, but she was one of those people—and there are a surprising number of them—who, when they are told they can't do a thing, immediately want to do it.

"Then I don't see why you shouldn't," said the man. "Perhaps you'd care to go round with me?"

Grace looked at him doubtfully. He seemed perfectly nice, but on the other hand she had strict instructions not to speak to strangers.

"Would you mind waiting just a minute?" she asked.

"I'm not a kidnapper," the man said mildly. "But I quite see your point. Perhaps this will help."

And he took a rather crumpled card out of his pocket and gave it to Grace. It said:

"S. Wilkins. Demonstrator. Simmonds—The Store That Has Everything."

Grace took the card and pulled the unwilling Griffin away from the postcards and just outside the door.

"I don't think it's fair," she whispered. "They don't say anything about No Griffins Admitted. But the point is shall I go with Mr Wilkins. Is he all right?"

"Right as a rain drop," the Griffin said cheerfully. "What sense of smell I do have left after the horrors of your polluted atmosphere tells me that. In actual fact this Wilkins has a most unusual scent. It is a strange mixture of some powerful cleanser and something which reminds me of the Good Old Days. The days when Creatures such as I . . ."

"Yes, yes, yes," said Grace hurriedly for she knew how the Griffin could run on if given half a chance. "But if I do go with him, what am I to look *for*?"

The Griffin scratched its ear thoughtfully.

"Approach one of the Temple Guards and enquire whether there are still any treasures unaccounted for in their beautiful store house."

"I couldn't," said Grace. "They'd think I was mad."

"If you don't," the Griffin replied, "I've a good mind to tell Joe about-you-know-what."

"Oh, all right," Grace said furiously. "But if I'm taken away and locked up it'll be all your fault."

"Are you worrying about your dog?" said Mr Wilkins who had got tired of waiting. "I'm sure he'll be all right. He's really a remarkably intelligent looking animal. He seems to understand every word you say."

"Oh, but he *does*," Grace replied, "Now stay here—er—Griff."

The Griffin sat down on the grass near Joe, and Grace and Mr Wilkins went back into the Pavilion and began to walk round it slowly. It was unlike any place Grace had ever seen, which was not surprising as it is in its way quite unique. Some people admire it enormously, while others call it vulgar and ridiculous, but to Grace it was all very beautiful, from its curious Chinese wallpaper to its great glittering chandeliers and golden furniture. Indeed, she got so carried away by it all that she almost forgot the Griffin's instructions.

Mr Wilkins stopped being sad and became very cheerful as he talked and talked about everything they saw.

"Do you think," said Grace suddenly, deciding that Mr Wilkins was far more likely to be understanding than the official attendants, "that there are any treasures unaccount—unaccounted for?"

"What a curious question," said Mr Wilkins.

"Somebody asked me to ask," mumbled Grace.

"Oh quite," said Mr Wilkins politely. "Yes, I dare say that some of the original pieces have gone astray Had you anything particular in mind?"

"Not really," said Grace, wishing that the Griffin had explained things better.

"It's a question that I've often asked myself," Mr Wilkins said dreamily. "Imagine how wonderful it would be to stumble across some lost treasure which once belonged to the Pavilion."

"Have you ever found any sort of treasure at all?" asked Grace.

"One or twice I have come across a few little things,"

Mr Wilkins admitted. They were out in the sunshine again by this time and Mr Wilkins blinked and looked about as though he couldn't remember for a moment where he was.

"Thank you very much for taking me round," Grace said politely.

Joe and the Griffin, who had been sitting ten feet apart on the grass not talking to each other, both got up and came over, and Grace introduced everybody. Mr Wilkins shook hands politely and said to Joe:

"Tell me, are you as interested in lost treasure as Grace is?"

"In a way," said Joe.

The Griffin trod heavily on his foot, and Joe added hurriedly:

"In fact, yes, I am."

Mr Wilkins looked at them thoughtfully and suddenly seemed to make up his mind about something.

"I tell you what," he said. "If you like, I could show you something which I really am rather proud of. Only it's my lunch hour and I haven't got much time left."

"But it's only half-past eleven," said Grace.

"What sort of thing?" Joe asked curiously.

Mr Wilkins lent forward and said in a low voice:

"One or two forgotten treasures."

# 7. *The Flying Rug*

Mr Wilkins lived in a narrow, noisy street at the back of the Clock Tower in a room above a grocery shop. He ushered the children up the dark stairs, and Grace kept a firm hold on the Griffin just to make quite sure that it didn't go away. But the Griffin seemed even more eager than Mr Wilkins to get to the room and really pushed its way quite rudely through the doorway. It was quite a big room as it turned out, but then there were a great many things in it: not ordinary things like tables and chairs, although it had those all right, but vases and pictures and books, and even a couple of stone statues.

"You will excuse me, won't you," said Mr Wilkins, "if I get on with my cooking for a moment, but I do get so terribly hungry about now."

He pulled aside a small curtain, and there was a tiny stove and a sink. He got an egg out of a cupboard, and Grace couldn't help noticing that there was hardly any food in it except for a very stale-looking loaf of bread and some margarine that had begun to melt.

"Is that all you're going to have?" asked Joe, thinking of the wonderful dinners that Mrs Chatter cooked for him.

"It's plenty," said Mr Wilkins earnestly. "As it happens you see, I'm saving up for something."

"What?" asked Grace before Joe could stop her.

"A Chinese plate," said Mr Wilkins happily, and he stood quite still for a moment with the egg in one hand and a saucepan in the other.

"I see," said Grace politely, although she didn't in the least, because buying a silly old plate instead of some proper food seemed a very odd thing to do. "Perhaps I could make you some toast."

"That would be kind," Mr Wilkins replied. "It always seems to burn when I do it. Bother, the gas is getting low. Never mind I'll go and put a shilling in the meter."

He hurried out of the room still holding the egg.

"Do you think he's got any Treasure?" Joe asked the Griffin in a low voice. "He doesn't look in the least rich to me."

"He's not the sort who cares for worldly appearances," the Griffin said. "But his taste's not half bad. Most of the stuff is damaged or cracked so it's not very valuable, but it's nice of its kind. I suppose you could call some of these objects Forgotten Treasure. We take them off our books naturally when they lose their value."

"Then what *you* want isn't here?" Joe asked.

"Oh, I wouldn't say that exactly," the Griffin replied, wandering round the room and sniffing. Its eyes had begun to glitter so that they looked like emeralds and its tail swung gently.

"Great Zeus!" it said so suddenly that both Joe and Grace jumped.

"What is it?" asked Grace, forgetting to watch the toast.

"Patience is a virtue," the Griffin said in a muffled voice as it burrowed underneath a rather tattered fire guard. "Here we come," and it slithered out again with a dusty mat between its teeth.

"It doesn't look like much to me," said Joe, who had been expecting at least a golden casket.

"It wouldn't," said the Griffin sneezing violently. "Well, well, well."

"It's only a dirty old rug," said Joe who, what with one thing and another, was now thoroughly out of sorts. He'd missed his bathe, he had spent half an hour outside the Pavilion with a sulky Griffin, and the smell of the toast was starting to make him feel hungry.

"*Dirty old rug!*" the Griffin said furiously. "Your ignorance is disgraceful. Does this texture mean nothing to you? Can you not read these symbols?"

It fairly danced about as it spoke, and as Joe was just about as angry as the creature, what might have happened next could have been most unfortunate, but luckily—or unluckily from Mr Wilkins' point of view—the toast chose this moment to catch fire. Grace flapped at it with both hands and the flames died down and all that was left was a black mess and a very strong smell of burning.

"I'll have to do him another piece," said Grace, hastily opening the window and throwing the burnt bits out, to the delight of several sparrows who had been bullied away from the seafront by a flock of gulls who were bigger and bossier than they were.

"Dirty old rug indeed," grumbled the Griffin. It spread the little mat out tenderly on the floor and brushed it with the tip of one shining wing. Dust flew in all directions, and Joe, whose anger had died down a little, was forced to admit that the rug was really quite handsome in an unusual sort of way. The pattern was faded and it looked more like a strange kind of writing than anything else.

"Turkish," said the Griffin, walking round and round it, and to Joe's astonishment it put down its head and laid one ear against the pile.

"What *are* you doing?" asked Grace who couldn't get on with the toast because the gas had now entirely disappeared.

"Listening," replied the Griffin shortly. "Tut, tut. What a very sad story. It makes one realise one should be grateful for one's own blessings however small."

"You mean the rug's talking to you?" said Joe. "That's impossible. I don't believe it."

"You'll be a grown-up one of these days," said the Griffin as though that was some terrible fate. "You'll never believe anything until your leaders have shaken it into you, and what is——"

"But what did it tell you?" Grace asked quickly.

"Its life story of course. Sold into bondage, abandoned, captured, sold again and finally condemned as worthless."

"*I* didn't hear anything," said Joe.

"*That* doesn't surprise me," the Griffin replied tartly. "And if you think it's so impossible, how do you explain the radio? The television? The——"

"That's different," said Joe.

"Hah!" replied the Griffin.

"Is it magic?" asked Grace hopefully.

"In a way," the Griffin said grudgingly. "I suppose you've heard of travelling carpets?"

Joe and Grace looked at the Griffin blankly. It stamped its foot in irritation.

"Magic carpets, then," it snapped.

Joe and Grace walked slowly across the room and stared at the rug as though they were afraid it might bite them.

"You're pulling our legs," Joe said uncertainly.

At this unfortunate and really rather rude remark the

Griffin lost its temper entirely. It put its head down and butted Joe painfully in the bend of the knees. Joe fell foward onto the rug before he could stop himself, and at the same moment, the Griffin whispered something to it. The rug quivered, straightened itself out and somewhat unsteadily rose off the ground with an astonished Joe clutching at its stiff edges.

"Put me down," shouted Joe as the mat sailed lazily round the room some eight feet off the ground. "Put me—ouch!" His head hit the ceiling, and the Griffin swung its tail with delight.

"Pulling your unworthy legs was I?" it said. "Telling you untruths? Oh unbelievers, oh miserable——"

"Dear, nice Griffin," said Grace, "we do believe you now, really we do, only please make it stop before Joe gets hurt."

"Not yet, I won't," the Griffin said.

Its bad temper had completely disappeared and so had its dignity. It pranced across the floor underneath the floating Joe with its head back and its eyes gleaming, while Grace dodged along behind it making grabs at the edge of the rug as it flew past.

"Not a bad performance eh?" said the Griffin. "A little rusty taking off perhaps, but that's hardly surprising considering it hasn't been used properly for some two thousand years. It's an export model, you know, woven for the Egyptian market. They made quite a lot of these little run-about-rugs at that time, and very popular they were, too, with the people who couldn't afford a full-size carpet. Why, I remember——"

"If you don't let me down," said Joe furiously as his shoulder hit the picture rail, "I'll never speak to you again. In fact, I'll tell the Civil Guard about you and—and—you'll be shown on television and they'll never let you go, so you'll never find your precious Treasure."

"Temper, temper," the Griffin said reprovingly.

"Somebody's coming," said Grace. "If Mr Wilkins sees Joe up there, he'll go mad."

The Griffin took a running leap off the ground, mumbled at the rug as it swept past and at the same moment the door opened and Mr Wilkins came in holding the egg. The rug and Joe landed at his feet, and Mr Wilkins backed up against the wall and shut his eyes.

"Excuse me," he said faintly. "It must be the sun, but for a moment I thought I saw—no that's impossible."

"You see," the Griffin whispered triumphantly in Joe's ear. "What did I tell you? Adults always blame this kind of thing on the weather."

"It's all right," Grace said gently. "Joe was only having a ride on your magic rug. You haven't really got sun-stroke."

Joe and the Griffin held their respective breaths and glared at her while they waited for Mr Wilkins to go rushing off after the nearest policeman. In fact, all he did was to pull a handkerchief out of his pocket and pat his forehead with it. Some of the colour came back into his face and he said in a dreamy voice:

"Thought transference, I suppose. Of course one's always more susceptible to these things when one is hungry." Then he opened his eyes, patted Grace on the head and handed her the egg. "I hope it was a nice game?" he said politely.

The Griffin came as near to a laugh as a Griffin can, and Joe got up off his knees and dusted some of the white plaster off his shoulders. He had left several rather dirty finger-marks on the ceiling, but he supposed that Mr Wilkins would never notice them. He was quite right. Mr Wilkins never did.

"But——" said Grace, and then much to Joe's relief she thought better of it and took the egg over to the stove to boil it.

"Sorry I was so long," said Mr Wilkins, "but I couldn't find a shilling. I'm one of those people who never seem to have the right money on them."

"I've known other people like that," Joe said, looking darkly at Grace.

It was really very strange, sitting there, watching Mr Wilkins have his lunch and being very ordinary, when only a few minutes before Joe had been floating round the room on a magic rug. But it was also rather reassuring because a little magic can go a very long way if you are not used to it.

After the last spoonful of egg and the last sip of tea had disappeared, Mr Wilkins rummaged round among his things and produced a somewhat dented little silver box with a rather odd-shaped lion embossed on the lid.

"I found this in a junk shop," hc said proudly. "It's one of my most prized possessions."

"It's very nice," said Grace politely, although she much preferred the little boxes with shells stuck round the edges and "A Present from Brighton" stamped on the lid.

"That's a Gryphon," said Mr Wilkins, pointing at the lion.

"Or Griffin," corrected Joe, "the hereditary Guardian of Treasures."

"I say," Mr Wilkins exclaimed. "That's jolly good. Did you learn it at school?"

"A friend told me," mumbled Joe. The Griffin which had shoved itself forward to have a look at its portrait, grunted, and Mr. Wilkins patted its golden head and pulled forward a blue bowl decorated with dragons.

"And that's early Japanese," he said. "Another real find even if it is cracked."

He seemed so pleased at having found someone to talk to about his treasures that Joe hadn't the heart to say it was time to go, and anyway he quite enjoyed himself because Mr Wilkins, once started, was full of interesting stories and pieces of information.

"I really have enjoyed our little talk," he said—although the children hadn't spoken a word—"but I really must get back to work now."

"We've enjoyed it too," said Grace, and the Griffin nodded.

"And what sort of treasure are you looking for?" Mr Wilkins asked as he put his things away again.

"We shan't really know till we see it," Joe said cautiously.

"I know just what you mean," Mr Wilkins said. He

glanced round the room and then added slowly, "You really admired the rug most, didn't you?"

"Oh *yes*," said Grace.

Mr Wilkins picked it up and stroked it, and when he spoke again it was as if he'd forgotten there was anybody else in the room.

"I remember," he said dreamily, "when I was a child I used to imagine I had a magic carpet. Of course I never did own one, but strangely enough this little rug brought back those memories very strongly. It's a great pity there's no such thing as magic." He sighed.

"But there *is*," Grace said earnestly.

Mr Wilkins smiled at her.

"Imagination's a wonderful gift," he said, "and I'm sure you and Joe will get far more out of this rug than I ever will, so I'd like you to have it."

There was a surprised silence, and the Griffin, which was afraid the opportunity might slip past if nobody did anything about it, lent across and gently pulled the rug out of Mr Wilkins' grasp.

"*What* an intelligent animal," Mr Wilkins said delightedly.

The Griffin tried to look bashful and failed completely.

"Are you sure you mean it?" asked Joe.

"Indeed I do. You've given me so much pleasure by listening to me rambling on, I should like to show my gratitude," said Mr Wilkins seriously.

"Thank you very much then," said Joe, and Grace seized Mr Wilkins' hand and shook it up and down.

"We'll find you a simply splendid treasure in return," she said.

"A magic treasure, of course," said Mr Wilkins, his eyes twinkling.

"Of course," agreed Grace, and Mr Wilkins laughed and led the way down the narrow, dark stairs and into the busy street.

"I do hope you'll call again," he said. "Any time. But now I simply must fly."

Joe half handed him the rug without thinking, and Mr Wilkins smiled again, but shook his head and went hurrying off between the slow-moving shoppers.

The others walked back to the Old Steine and caught the Number 7a for Kemp Town and were lucky enough to get the top deck all to themselves.

"We're going to be jolly late for lunch," said Joe.

"Who cares," said Grace who was feeling very happy—after all it's not every day that somebody makes you a present of a flying carpet, even if it is only a Small Export Model.

"It's all right for you," said Joe, "with all your servants to look after you, but Mrs Chatter gets quite ratty if I'm not on time."

"Peace between you," said the Griffin which was lying across one seat having a quiet whisper with the rug. "Neither of you is going home to a tin of Woof-Woof. You should be grateful for that."

"Was Mr Wilkins any good to you?" asked Joe.

"He didn't guard that which I am seeking," the Griffin replied thoughtfully. "But his dwelling was a resting-place, nay a haven in this alien world in which I now find myself. I will go further and say . . ."

"Not if I can help it," Joe whispered to Grace. He added more loudly:

"Yes, but was there a sniff of your Treasure there?"

"No," the Griffin said simply, "but I'd like to check on one or two of the things he has got when I return to my Account Books. All damaged, of course. Alas, the list grows ever longer." It sighed deeply.

"Never mind," Grace said gently, "we have got the rug. You'd better look after that, Joe. My—er—my . . .'

"Slaves?" prompted the Griffin, opening one green eye and looking at her. Grace cleared her throat.

"—might not like it," she said quickly.

"All right," Joe agreed. "Well, what shall we do this afternoon? Bathe?"

"I can't come out," Grace said regretfully, "I'm doing something else."

"And I desire time and peace in which to think," said the Griffin. "There are so many cross-currents in this case. I seem to catch a whiff—and then it's gone." It scratched its ear thoughtfully.

"Where are you going?" asked Joe.

"The Regal-Splendide Hotel, actually," said Grace. "I expect you know it."

"Only by sight," replied Joe.

And indeed there is hardly anybody in Brighton who cannot say the same. It is an extremely large and very expensive hotel, where, so it is said, they charge five shillings for just one cup of tea without the pot.

Grace could have said a lot more, but at that moment the conductor shouted up the stairs:

"Royal Sussex 'ospital."

"See you tomorrow then," gabbled Joe. He picked up the rug and, with the Griffin at his heels, bolted off down the stairs. He ran all the way to Mulliner Terrace, but, as it happened, by some extraordinary coincidence Mrs Chatter had been delayed in getting the lunch so he wasn't late at all.

The Griffin could probably have explained why this should be so, but it didn't bother because it naturally took magic for granted while Joe still hadn't got the hang of it at all.

# 8. *The Mounted Policeman*

MRS CHATTER didn't seem to mind Joe bringing home the rug although she did say that he shouldn't go round talking to strangers. So Joe tried to explain how nice Mr Wilkins was, and Mrs Chatter, instead of reading him a lecture about taking a present from somebody he hardly knew, only laughed and said she hoped the rug hadn't got moth in it.

"You'd better give it a good spray with Puffo," she said. "Now hurry up, do, because I'm all behind like the lamb's tail and I've got a pile of laundry to wash."

"Would you like me to stay and mangle?" asked Joe, who was feeling quite himself again after sausage and mash and two helpings of cherry tart.

"On a lovely afternoon like this? I should think not, indeed," said Mrs Chatter. "Just go up and get Mr Serafin's tray for me, would you, dear?"

Joe took the rug up to the first floor front, and Mr Serafin instead of sitting in front of the window and going to sleep for half an hour as he usually did, was getting out his panama hat.

"Very handsome, Joe," he said, admiring the rug. "Fancy you liking something like that, though. I thought you collected space guns and plastic soldiers."

"That was when I was younger," Joe said.

"I beg your pardon I'm sure," said Mr Serafin gravely. "Well I think I'll just try and toddle down to the Front and back."

"I thought the Trouble in your Legs wouldn't let you," said Joe.

"S'funny thing," said Mr Serafin, brushing up his hat on the sleeve of his coat. "But ever since the day those two boys set on you, Joe, and I chased them off, the Trouble seems to have got less and less. Touch wood."

He and Joe both touched the table for a moment, and the Griffin watched them with astonishment.

"I'm jolly glad," said Joe, picking up the tray whose plates were so clean they hardly looked as if they'd been used at all.

"Not half as glad as I am," said Mr Serafin winking. "See you later, alligator," and he shuffled off quite briskly, considering how fat he was.

Half an hour later, Joe and the Griffin found themselves walking off down Mulliner Terrace towards Black Rock. The Griffin waited till the street was empty and then said in a puzzled voice.

"This touching of wooden objects—is it some form of religious rite to ward off evil spirits?"

"Oh no," said Joe. "You just do it for luck."

"Give me patience," murmured the Griffin. "And the word to toddle? What does that mean?"

"To walk," translated Joe, "like a baby, really."

"It's a new one on me," the Griffin said, "and very ugly, too. And who was this alligator to which Mr Serafin referred?"

"It's just a saying," said Joe. "And it's terribly old-fashioned really. Mr Serafin's slang usually is. I should have replied, 'in a while, crocodile,' or, 'see you soon, macaroon,' or . . ."

"Stop," commanded the Griffin. "Your chants are completely meaningless to me."

Joe did as he was asked, and the two of them walked in silence all the way to where the pavement gently turns itself into a path which leads up to the Downs and the golf course which overlooks the housing estate of Whitehawk.

The Griffin padded along the grass verge until they came to the place where it flattened out, and then the Griffin stopped and gazed out over the neat curving streets, the fat gasometers and the high blocks of flats.

"And to think I can remember when it was only a Roman camp," it said rather sadly. "Makes you feel your age."

"What was it like?" Joe asked curiously.

"Not unlike this, strangely enough. They were a very orderly lot, the Romans, I will say that for them. Everything on the square and done by numbers. But they used to get terribly homesick, poor chaps."

"For—for Rome?"

"Not really. Quite a lot of them didn't come from the Capital at all; they were country lads conscripted into the army. No, what they really missed was the climate and the nice oily food and the Italian wine. They were always going sick with 'flu—Britons Ague they called it—or colds or rheumatism or something, but really it was only homesickness. I was tracking down a couple of Golden Eagles at the time. They'd been pinched by a local tribe of Ancient Britons from over Rottingdean way. We had quite a struggle getting them back. They thought they were some kind of tribal gods, you see. And so they were in a way, I suppose. Oh well . . ."

"Fancy," said Joe, just like Mr Serafin. He had learnt a bit about the Romans at school, of course, but they had always seemed rather boring to him until this moment, and now, just for a moment, it seemed to Joe as if the whole world were holding its breath and that the Romans of two thousand years ago were still alive and that everything was really happening at once.

"Isn't history odd . . ." said Joe, and stopped.

"You're learning," the Griffin said nodding. "I never thought you would, but you are."

Then everything went on as usual, and there was only a small boy and an odd-shaped ugly dog out for a walk on the sunny Downs.

Joe waited until they had found a spot under a chalky bank near the golf course, and then he unrolled the rug and lay down on it while the Griffin stretched out alongside and closed its emerald eyes. But it wasn't asleep, for Joe could see its long tail twitching every now and again so he knew it was only thinking deeply and thoughtfully kept quiet himself.

"I dunno," the Griffin said at last when Joe was almost dozing off. "It's like the conjuring tricks the Persian magicians used to play. Now you see it, now you don't. Once or twice I've caught a distinct sniff of the Treasure, but it keeps getting overlaid with other scents."

"I expect it's the petrol fumes," Joe said helpfully. The Griffin was a trial in many ways and often quite dangerous, but he didn't like to see it getting downhearted.

"I shall triumph in the end," the Griffin said, getting up and stretching. "I always do, but time runs on, alas."

It scratched on the chalky soil with one sharp claw as though it was doing sums. Joe leant over and watched, but he couldn't make head or tail of it, and the Griffin suddenly wiped out the whole lot and yawned widely.

"You need not reproach yourself," it said kindly, although Joe had no intention of doing any such thing. "You have done your best, limited though your powers are, and, like the Understanding Wilkins, I should like to reward you a little for your goodness."

"I say, look here," mumbled Joe, "there's no need . . ."

"Don't chatter, boy," the Griffin said. "Perhaps I *was* a little hard on you this morning. It was the excitement and one thing and another. How about a little ride, eh?"

The Griffin sounded so exactly like a kind elderly uncle offering a treat that it made Joe smile.

"That's better," the Griffin said. "I remember when I was quite young myself we used to give the children of the Temple Guards a little spin now and again while their mothers were out shopping in the market."

"Didn't the mothers mind?" asked Joe.

He hadn't got one himself now, but he couldn't imagine someone like Mrs Chatter taking it very calmly if he went flying off over the Eye Hospital while she was round at the Self-Service.

"They never knew," the Griffin said simply. "Some of the smaller children used to tell their parents all about it, of course, but they always thought it was just a game. Grown-ups have changed hardly at all in the few thousand years that I've known them. More's the pity."

"Yes, but look here," said Joe, frowning horribly because he was thinking so hard. "I'm me now and I know you're a Griffin and that this is a magic rug and I'll still know that when I'm older, and so will Grace."

"Ah, but you won't *believe* it," the Griffin replied, shaking a golden claw at Joe. "You'll tell yourselves that it was all just a splendid game you thought up for your own amusement. I daresay you'll even refer to me as 'that handsome and remarkable dog' you once knew which was so much more intelligent, brave, trustworthy——"

"Quite," said Joe hurriedly. "OK. Let's have a go then."

"I wish I knew who was this Okie to whom you so constantly make your salutations," the Griffin said. "There was a certain character in Norse mythology I recall—still, we won't go into that now as I never cared for him. Now then, on you get and don't fidget."

"Not too high now," Joe said nervously, sitting down on the rug and gripping it firmly with both hands.

"So be it," agreed the Griffin, and so it was, for this time the rug only lifted a few inches off the ground, and it was a very pleasant feeling to go sliding through the air with no effort. In fact, there are really few nicer ways of spending an afternoon on your own than with a magic carpet however small. Joe soon became quite used to it and asked the Griffin if he could go up a little further.

The Griffin obligingly whispered to the rug, and Joe rose several feet up in the clear sunny air so that he could see right across the golf course and out to the sparkling sea.

"It's smashing," shouted Joe.

"Relax, not so stiff," replied the Griffin trotting along behind.

"Higher," ordered Joe.

"I suppose it's all right," the Griffin said doubtfully, looking round, but it took to its wings, and swooping up alongside the rug whispered to it again.

Away shot Joe, hanging on for all he was worth while the Griffin flapped beside him a trifle breathlessly for it was very out of practice and getting a bit fat. Joe was so excited that he never noticed the golfer coming towards him until it was far too late. Just for a moment he glimpsed a fat red face with its mouth wide open, and then he was over the man's head and gliding towards the next bunker.

"Oh my," said the golfer feebly. The Griffin made a really very graceful half turn, swooped down on him and said quite pleasantly:

"And who said he was going to the office this afternoon?"

The golfer shut both his mouth and his eyes, and when he opened them again he was all alone apart from the skylarks.

"It's a judgement on me," the man said, sitting down and putting his head in his hands. "I shouldn't have eaten that big dinner last night, or come out without my hat, or told lies about going to the office. Conscience, that's what it was. Conscience. I'll never do it again."

Right there and then he picked up his golf clubs and walked back to the club house where he'd left his car. He drove straight home and told his wife he hadn't been to work at all. As it happened she knew that already, but she was a wise woman and held her tongue and gave her husband three cups of tea with plenty of sugar in them. After that he only played golf at the weekends and always took his wife with him because he was frightened he might have another attack of bad indigestion and so start seeing things. But, of course, he never did.

Meanwhile a very scared Joe had been set down by the rug which he hurriedly rolled up and put under his arm.

"Your world is so crowded," complained the Griffin. "People everywhere. It's every bit as bad as Atlantis, and they had a really shocking overpopulation problem."

"Supposing that man reports us to the police?" Joe asked.

"He won't," the Griffin replied smiling to itself.

But Joe wasn't nearly so sure, and he began to walk very fast indeed down the chalky path that lead back to Kemp Town. He had just reached the road when there was a clip-clopping noise behind him. Joe turned round and there, coming straight for him, was a mounted policeman.

"Cripes," said Joe, and took to his heels.

So naturally the policeman, who had hardly noticed him before, thought he had been up to something and tapped his heels against the sides of the horse. Of course Joe should have known better than to run, but he was very frightened and in no time at all the policeman had overtaken him.

"Now then, sonny," he said, "what are you doing, eh?"

"Nothing," stuttered Joe, almost dropping the rug in his agitation.

"And what's that?" the policeman said, far more sternly.

"A r–r–rug," said Joe.

"I think I'd better have a look at it," the policeman was beginning when a really terrible thing happened, for the Griffin, which had stopped to take some burrs out of its golden coat, came round the corner and saw the horse. The horse saw the Griffin too and both creatures stiffened at once.

The Griffin's mixture of fur and feathers stood up on end, its tail went quite straight and its green eyes narrowed down to gleaming slits.

"Rrrrrrrrrrrr," it said.

The horse put back its ears, rolled its eyes and trembled so violently that the mounted policeman almost fell off.

"Steady boy, steady," he said.

But the horse took no notice at all and skittered round and round in the road on stiff legs while the Griffin crouched down and prepared to spring at it.

Both the policeman and Joe were extremely worried for entirely different reasons. What neither of them knew was that Griffins are the traditional enemies of all horses, and all horses, of course, are very aware of this. This particular horse had been most carefully trained to take no notice of traffic or crowds or sudden noises of any kind, but nobody had told it how to behave when faced with a Griffin.

At the same moment as the Griffin prepared to spring, the horse quite literally took the bit between its teeth and bolted for all it was worth down the road towards Rottingdean, taking its rider with it.

"Stop, oh stop," shouted Joe, and very bravely flung his arms round the Griffin's neck—bravely, because that creature looked quite different from its usual haughty self, and very frightening indeed. It tried to shake Joe off, but Joe refused to be shaken, and after a moment or so it stopped growling and its coat lay down again.

"I crave your indulgence," it said a trifle hoarsely. "A fit of pure madness. But the fact is I can't stand horses."

"Now you *have* done it," said Joe, letting go and staring after the policeman who was just vanishing over the brow of the hill, looking for all the world as if he were taking part in a race.

"Oh no I haven't," replied the Griffin smoothing out its ruffled wings. "He'll never tell anyone what happened because it wouldn't look good for his horse. We'll never see *that* Civil Guard again I can promise you."

Which, as it happened, was quite untrue, for they did see that particular policeman again and under the most unfortunate circumstances.

## *9. Very White Magic*

QUITE understandably, Joe had been considerably shaken up by his meeting with the mounted policeman, and he decided that he was going to have no more adventures, with or without magic, for the time being.

"I call it very poor spirited of you," the Griffin said, but it wasn't too keen on going out again for a while itself, and was quite happy to lie out in the back garden talking softly to the rug which Mrs Chatter had insisted on spraying with Puffo.

Luckily Grace made a very good audience for all Joe's tales of woe and, although she rather regretted not having a ride on the rug herself, she did see Joe's point that they could hardly go out with it now when probably half the police force of Brighton were searching for it.

"Never mind," Grace said kindly, "I'll tell you about what happened to me at the hotel. We had——"

"We?" asked Joe.

"There were quite a few of us," Grace said airily. "But everybody else was grown-up," she added in case Joe should feel hurt at being left out.

"Well, what did you have?" prompted Joe, tickling Tiger behind the ears. Tiger had become a great deal more affectionate since the arrival of the Griffin. Perhaps he was a little jealous.

"Cream puffs and sardine sandwiches and salmon sandwiches and sausage rolls and chocolate cake and strawberry tarts and sugar biscuits and three different sorts of ice cream and fruit salad and jellies and . . ." she paused for breath, "and fizzy orange to drink."

"Goodness," said Joe, very much impressed.

"Oh, they always have food like that at the Regal-Splendide," said Grace. "I think I liked the salmon best. It was the most expensive sort, you know. But what are we going to do now? We can't go searching for

Treasure on our own when we don't know what it looks like, can we?"

But that problem was solved for them by Mr Serafin suddenly puffing out into the little garden, a thing he had never done before, and offering them each a shrimping net.

"I saw them down at the little shop on the Lower Prom," he said, lowering himself onto a kitchen chair and keeping his feet well away from the Griffin.

"You went all the way down there?" Joe asked in astonishment.

"That's right," agreed Mr Serafin. "I haven't enjoyed a toddle so much in years. I'm thinking of taking the bus up to Portslade next week to watch the bowls match."

"How lovely," said Grace, who privately thought that it was a very dull way of enjoying oneself. "And thank you very much for the nets. Perhaps we'll catch you a mackerel for your tea."

"That'd be nice," said Mr Serafin.

But all they did get was a very small crab which Grace insisted on throwing back into the sea, and a large assortment of weeds, pebbles and shells. But once you have started searching for something, even if it's only something like shrimps and not a Valuable Treasure, it is very difficult to stop, and as the Griffin seemed perfectly content to stay at home and guard the rug—for, as it so rightly said, it didn't feel really happy unless it was guarding something—the days went past very happily and quickly.

Until, that is, the unfortunate afternoon when Joe stretched just too far to try and reach a crab and lost his footing and fell into three feet of sea. He climbed out again all right, but he was wearing his best trousers at the time as his other pair had got a big tear in them from a rock the day before, and Joe, as he went wetly home, knew there was going to be Trouble—and there was.

"What have you done?" demanded Mrs Chatter, which wasn't very fair of her as anybody could see exactly what Joe had done as he stood dripping all over the kitchen floor.

"They'll dry," said Joe hopefully.

"Oh, they'll dry all right," Mrs Chatter said darkly. "And a pretty picture they'll look all covered in slime and goodness knows what else. Now if only I had a washing machine . . ."

It was quite obviously the end of the shrimping season, at least for a while, so Joe and Grace stacked the nets neatly away in the kitchen passage and tried to think of a way of cheering up Mrs Chatter.

"Why not make her a gift showing your love and affection?" the Griffin suggested helpfully.

"It's not her birthday," said Joe.

"All the more reason then," replied the Griffin. "Don't be so tight pursed."

"It's all very well for you to talk," Joe said hotly. "You just steal things, but if you must know I'm broke."

"Where?" the Griffin asked with interest. It got up and padded across the garden and stared at Joe, who forgot his bad temper and laughed instead.

"Broke means no money," he explained, "like stony-broke. You know."

"Slang, English Usage of, Volume Twenty-Six," the Griffin said absently. "Yes, of course. It had slipped my mind for the moment. Well then, make Mrs Chatter something. Don't give up so easily, boy."

Joe had done some carpentry at school, but he hadn't got any tools in Mulliner Terrace, or any wood come to that, so he wasn't getting along very fast when Grace, who had been listening to the conversation with a rather uncomfortable expression on her face, suggested sticking some of the shells they had collected round the edge of a mirror.

"It'll look ever so pretty, really it will," she said to Joe, who felt doubtful, but as he hadn't got any better ideas himself he gave in. Luckily Grace was able to supply a piece of mirror and while she painted the shells Joe made the glue which he really rather enjoyed. The present when finished was a little smudged, and too late everybody noticed that so many shells had been stuck round it you could hardly see your face at all, but Mrs Chatter was delighted.

"I do call that nice," she said several times, and Joe was rather afraid she was going to try and kiss him so he hurriedly backed behind the kitchen table.

"And now I'll give *you* a treat," Mrs Chatter said, putting the mirror up on the mantelpiece. "They're having an extra special demonstration down at Simmonds. We'll go to that and then have a proper Fancy Tea afterwards."

Joe didn't particularly want to go, but Grace seemed just as keen on the idea as Mrs Chatter, so he didn't really have much say in the matter. Grace came back promptly after lunch, and Joe, who had struggled unwillingly into a clean shirt and his best trousers (which had shrunk a little because they had been boiled), took her into the garden where the Griffin was talking to Tiger.

"What is this Simmonds?" it asked.

"Simmonds, the Store That Has Everything," said Grace, who had often seen those words on the sides of paper bags.

"Everything?" said the Griffin.

"Everything," Grace replied firmly. "They've got toys and clothes and food and——"

"I wonder," interrupted the Griffin. "If it has Everything it may well contain my Treasure. Why didn't you tell me about it before, Joe? Really, I've no patience with you."

"It's no good getting cross with me," Joe said hotly, "because it's not at all the kind of place you'd find Treasure in. It's all ladies' dresses and bath salts and silly hats."

"Now then, now then," said Mr Serafin putting his head through the kitchen window. "Fix your mind on the Fancy Tea afterwards, Joe."

"I wish *you* were coming," said Joe, who didn't much like the idea of being the only male at the demonstration.

"All right, I will," said Mr Serafin, and vanished back inside the house.

"And so will I," said the Griffin.

So ten minutes later it was really quite a large party which climbed on board the 7a bus and headed for the Old Steine. Joe and Grace and the Griffin went upstairs.

"Isn't this fun?" said Grace.

"I should have thought it was pretty ordinary for you," replied Joe. "I mean you go to places like the Regal-Splendide and you've got a big house, and slave—that is servants, and everything."

"Yes, but this makes a nice change," Grace said quickly.

The Griffin laughed softly as though it was enjoying a private joke. Grace fidgeted. Lately she had seemed to have something on her mind, but Joe had enough problems of his own without taking on Grace's too. Besides it seemed to him that if you are a millionaire and live in a large house and eat your meals off silver plate there can't be many things which are a real worry.

Quite a lot of people were going into Simmonds, and Joe's spirits sank still further. He would far rather have been out shrimping or having a ride on the rug, and then, far too late to do anything about it, he remembered he'd left the rug all by itself in the garden. If it rained, would the magic run like water paints?

"I say," Joe whispered to the Griffin, but that creature was far too interested in what was going on around him to notice.

"What a store house," it murmured. "What delicious scents and potions. This place reminds me of the Palace of King Tikki-Ras, the All-powerful-one."

"It's only bath salts at one-and-six a bag," Joe said crushingly.

"I wish I could have some," said Grace.

"So you shall, lovey," said Mrs Chatter, who was getting quite carried away by the thought of watching the Superslic Washing Machine at work, and she bought Grace a bag of bright purple bath salts right there and then. Grace went very red in the face and looked as if she were going to cry, so Mr Serafin, who hated tears just as much as Joe did, pushed them on quickly towards a notice which said:

*Superslic This Way.*

"What riches," whispered the Griffin, bounding forwards, and immediately a man in a black coat and striped trousers (it was actually Mr Simmonds himself) put out a hand and said loudly:

"No dogs admitted unless on a lead."

"We'll wait outside then," Joe said quickly.

"Indeed you won't," replied Mrs Chatter, "I'll get him one now."

She hurried away with the Griffin at her heels, leaving the rest of her party to squeeze themselves into the demonstration show room which was filling up rapidly. Mr Serafin managed to capture four little gilt chairs at the end of a row and by the time everybody had sat themselves down—and Mr Serafin's chair creaked quite a lot when he did so—Mrs Chatter was back with the Griffin. It was wearing a green leather collar attached to a long lead and looked extremely pleased with itself.

"Isn't this nice?" said Mrs Chatter.

"Yes," said Joe dutifully, and looked at the Superslic

with loathing. It was very large and white and gleaming. He glanced down at the Griffin, and that creature put its great ugly head on his knee and looked up at him exactly like an ordinary dog.

"What's up?" whispered Grace.

"It's this magic business," Joe replied frowning. "Sometimes it seems realer than all this, but now this seems more real. Do you see what I mean?"

"Not really," Grace whispered back. Joe folded his arms and gave up trying to work it all out. Everybody was talking at once, and it was getting hotter and hotter and he was beginning to feel quite sleepy when Mr Simmonds walked up onto the little stage and lifted his hands for silence. The noise died away slowly.

"Ladies and gentlemen," he said, smiling so widely that Joe could see all his teeth, "—and I'm glad to know that some of you ladies have managed to get your husbands to come along this afternoon——"

There was some laughter, and the few men in the audience including Mr Serafin and Joe shifted about uncomfortably. Mr Simmonds laughed louder than anyone and then went on:

"This is a very special afternoon for Simmonds The Store That Has Everything."

"Humph," the Griffin said distinctly, and several people turned round to look at it. The Griffin shut its eyes, and Joe nudged it to keep quiet.

"A very special afternoon, because we are going to see this magnificent new washing machine in action. What it will do for your laundry, ladies, is pure magic."

Joe just managed to get his hand over the Griffin's mouth before it could say anything. It bit his finger gently and its tail thumped the floor.

"And what is more," Mr Simmonds went on staring hard at Joe, "there is a competition which you can all go in for, and the lucky winner will get a Superslic FREE."

Everybody clapped, and Mrs Chatter went quite pale with excitement.

"Oh, Joe, if only I *could* win," she said. "It would be the most wonderful thing that has ever happened to me."

"Perhaps you will," said Joe, although without much hope. He and Mrs Chatter had gone in for all kinds of competitions in the past and they had never even won so much as a set of wooden spoons.

"Does she really wish to acquire that—that monstrous object?" the Griffin said rather wetly into Joe's hand. Joe bent down and fiddled with his shoe so that his head was close to the Griffin's.

"That's right," he said softly.

"I shall never understand humans," said the Griffin, "not if I live to be *ten* thousand."

"Shhh," said Joe and Mr Simmonds together. Mr Simmonds had come up behind them very quietly and was now almost standing on the Griffin's tail. He bent over Mrs Chatter and smiled at her with all his teeth.

"I must ask you, madam, to keep your dog under control," he said.

"It's my fault," Joe said quickly, "I was the one who was talking."

The people in the row behind all laughed as if he'd said something amusing, but Mr Serafin promptly turned round and stared at them and they all hastily looked away again.

"Funny little chap," said Mr Simmonds in the kind of voice which showed he meant quite the opposite. "And now, ladies and gentlemen, silence for Simmonds' own Demonstrator."

The curtains at the side of the platform parted and on walked a familiar figure in a blue suit.

"It's Mr Wilkins," Grace said loudly.

"The Understanding Wilkins, so it is," agreed the Griffin. Luckily Mr Simmonds had moved on, but Joe, who was scared he might come back, said fiercely:

"If you don't behave yourself I'll—take you home."

The Griffin took no notice of this threat whatsoever. It shot a very disagreeable look at Mr Simmonds and then transferred its attention to Mr Wilkins who was starting to fiddle about with the washing machine. He looked rather miserable. The Griffin's ears went up and its green eyes shone, but only Joe noticed this and he experienced the now familiar sinking feeling in his middle which meant Trouble was coming.

What happened during the next half an hour was something that nobody was ever quite able to explain afterwards. Several people talked knowledgeably about conjuring and mass hypnotism while others contented themselves with the thought that they must have dozed off for forty winks and dreamt the whole business. It could all have been explained, of course, if anybody had thought of asking Joe and Grace, but nobody did and those two wisely kept their mouths very firmly closed indeed.

"Ladies and gentlemen," said Mr Wilkins in a rather muffled voice, "I'm proud to demonstrate for you this superb washing machine. The water comes in through this pipe here."

And even as he spoke the water did come through, although he hadn't touched the taps which controlled the pipe.

"We—we add a little Whiteo," said Mr Wilkins, gulping and reaching for the packet of detergent, but before he could reach it the packet floated across and emptied the powder into the machine of its own accord. Several people in the audience gasped and Mr Wilkins shut his eyes for a moment.

"Well done," shouted Mr Serafin. "Splendid, splendid!"

"And the water bubbles up immediately," Mr Wilkins said hoarsely.

Up it did indeed bubble, in a great frothy sea which billowed gently over the top of the machine and then slid down the sides so that Mr Wilkins looked as if he was standing in a shimmering cloud.

"Bravo, bravo. It's better than the Hippodrome," roared Mr Serafin, stamping his feet on the ground in his excitement and narrowly missing his panama hat.

"And then we put in the dirty laundry," Mr Wilkins said wildly, lunging for the basket which held the clothes, but he was far too late for it was already floating gently across the stage. It hovered for a moment over the

Superslic, then tilted upwards and the laundry cascaded into the frothing bubbles.

"The Superslic's washing action stops tangling," gabbled Mr Wilkins, "and it is safe for even the flimsiest clothing."

A lacy shawl promptly rose out of the bubbles and hung delicately in the air to show everybody it was all right. It turned round twice and then sank back once more. Most of the audience was now on its feet clapping as loudly as Mr Serafin. Other shoppers in the store, attracted by the noise, all made for the demonstration show room and tried to push their way through the doorway.

"Stop it, stop it," Joe implored the Griffin desperately. The creature shook its head.

"Not likely," it said. "I haven't enjoyed myself so much in years. The annual carnival in Troy was nothing compared to this, I promise you."

"Isn't it wonderful?" said Mrs Chatter, clasping her hands together.

"Time's up," said Mr Wilkins who's face was now as white as the bubbles surrounding him. He had his finger already on the switch to press it down, so he felt it quite clearly when the switch went on by itself.

"I'm dreaming of course," Mr Wilkins said to himself. "I've often wondered in the past if the day would come when these machines would run themselves and now I'm finding out what it would be like. Oh well, if it is only a dream I may as well enjoy it. In fact I'll see just how far it *will* go."

He stepped back, and folded his arms.

"Rinsing water," ordered Mr Wilkins.

The washing machine promptly obeyed and the bubbles immediately disappeared with little soapy plops, even the ones on the floor, and in came the fresh water.

"The last rinse," said Mr Wilkins, becoming as excited as his audience, "will leave your wash as clean as—as the ocean deeps."

The water instantly turned a faint shade of green and a slight but very pleasant smell of ozone filled the air.

"Ladies and gentlemen—the cleanest wash you have ever seen," said Mr Wilkins, flinging his arms wide. The machine hummed and stopped and out of its inside rose the laundry. Shirts, blouses, pyjamas, overalls and the shawl arranged themselves in a neat line as though they were already hanging in somebody's back garden and then gravely bowed to the audience. They were so clean it almost hurt to look at them. There was complete silence for a minute and then a great roar of applause.

Mr Wilkins and the laundry bowed modestly.

"Show us some more," somebody shouted.

"Try my hat," bellowed Mr Serafin and he tossed his old panama over the heads of the clapping people. It swerved and plopped into the machine. He got it back ten seconds later looking smarter than it had done when he had bought it. It was also bone dry.

Immediately there was an absolute stampede as everybody pressed forwards tearing off ties and scarves and waving handkerchiefs.

"Oh my, oh my," whispered Mrs Chatter, "oh *my*!"

"Do let's leave," implored Joe.

"Now," agreed Grace, who was just as frightened as he was as to what the Griffin might do next. She seized Mr Serafin's arm, and Joe took hold of Mrs Chatter's coat with one hand and the Griffin's lead with the other. They had a hard struggle to escape for now there were dozens of other people all fighting to get in.

"The competition," said Mrs Chatter grabbing at her hat which had been pushed over one eye, "I must get an entry form."

"There," replied Joe, pushing with all his might. "The man in the black coat, he's got them."

They shoved and heaved their way across to him. His eyes had rather a glazed expression, but he was smiling from ear to ear and handing out the printed forms as fast as he could go.

"I must congratulate you," said Mr Serafin, planting himself squarely in the way and refusing to be pushed out of it. "That's the best demonstration I've ever seen. Tell me, how *was* it done?"

"That's a trade secret," Mr Simmonds said, speaking more truthfully than he realised. The Griffin coughed gently to itself. "I'm so glad you enjoyed it, sir."

"It was quite remarkable," said Mr Serafin. "That demonstrator chap could make a fortune in the theatre. You were lucky to get him here."

"Oh quite," Mr Simmonds said rather uncomfortably, for the fact was that he had never thought very highly of Mr Wilkins and was on the point of asking him to leave.

"Double his pay or you'll lose him," the Griffin said in a deep voice.

Mr Simmonds smiled vaguely at Mr Serafin, and Joe hastily bundled Mrs Chatter outside. He didn't wait to see if the others were following him, but made off as fast as he could for Polly's Tea Parlour in West Street.

Joe and the Griffin arrived a couple of minutes ahead of the rest of the party, and Joe spent most of this in telling the Griffin exactly what he thought of it. The Griffin shrugged.

"That was nothing," it said. "Did I ever tell you about the time in Rome when . . ."

Then Mr Serafin came puffing up, and much to Joe's relief the Griffin stopped talking. They went inside and sat down, and Mrs Chatter, still flushed with excitement, said they could order anything they liked.

"Well, thank goodness that's over," said Joe when he and Grace had both finished their mixed grills and were trying to decide which cakes to have.

"I must say the bubbles were rather fun," Grace said.

"There's something I ought to tell you," the Griffin whispered against Joe's knee.

"Well don't," Joe whispered back. "You've done enough damage for one day."

"Oh all right then," the Griffin said huffily. "Only don't blame me when you find out what's happened, that's all."

It lay down and went to sleep all over Joe's feet, quite worn out from using so much magic in one afternoon.

# 10. *Tiger Takes a Trip*

QUITE a lot of things happened because of the Griffin taking such a liking to Mr Wilkins. First of all Simmonds sold every single Superslic they had, and secondly Mr Simmonds himself took Mr Wilkins out to lunch and called him 'my dear boy' every other sentence and offered him quite a lot more money to stay on with the store. Not double wages as the Griffin had suggested because, after thinking things over, Mr Simmonds had decided against anything quite so rash, but a sizeable amount all the same.

"Look here, there's something you ought to know," Mr Wilkins said. "You see, I didn't——"

"My dear boy," interrupted Mr Simmonds, "Simmonds needs men like you."

"Yes, but the demonstration wasn't anything to do with me, I mean . . ."

"Think it over, my dear boy," said Mr Simmonds, "and let me know definitely by the end of the week." He lowered his voice. "I suppose you wouldn't care to tell me exactly how it *was* done?"

"That's the whole point. I can't," Mr Wilkins said truthfully.

"Quite so. Well, my dear boy, it was a great success and to show how we appreciate your little effort you'll find something extra in your pay packet this week."

"But it wasn't *me*," said Mr Wilkins, rubbing his knuckles together in his agitation. "*I* didn't do it. It must have been done by someone in the audience. I thought I was dreaming at the time you see and . . ."

But Mr Simmonds had caught sight of an old and valued customer on the other side of the restaurant and was bowing and smiling at her and paying no attention to Mr Wilkins at all. So Mr Wilkins gave it up as a bad job, and when he got his extra money on Friday he spent it all on the Chinese plate for which he'd been trying to save up for weeks and weeks. It hadn't got a single crack or chip, and Mr Wilkins was so delighted with it he completely forgot to buy any food and had to live on boiled eggs for the entire weekend.

And the third thing was that Joe told the Griffin very, very firmly that it was never to do such a thing again.

"Poof," said the Griffin. "Don't you go ordering *me* about. *I* can do what I please."

"Not while you're in my—I mean Mrs Chatter's house —you can't," Joe replied sternly.

What with one thing and another Joe had really changed quite a lot during the holidays. He had always been rather a shy, timid boy, but life with the Griffin had been so full of difficult and even frightening situations that Joe had been forced to become braver in order to deal with them. He sounded so firm now, and looked so determined, that the Griffin was rather impressed, but it wouldn't have shown this for the world.

"Don't nag," it said. "Nobody knew it was me and anyway I had to teach that Simmonds a lesson. 'The Store That Has Everything' indeed! Why, there wasn't a whiff of Treasure in the whole place."

Joe opened his mouth to say "I told you so" and then thought better of it. Instead, he stretched himself out on the bedroom floor and stared at the competition form for the Superslic which Mrs Chatter had given him.

The Griffin stopped admiring itself in the glass and went across to have a look too.

"What do you want most in a washing machine?" it read out. "What a silly question."

"There are eleven more of them," Joe said, rubbing his pen through his hair, "and they get sillier all the time. Honestly it's worse than homework."

"Shift yourself," the Griffin said, sinking down on its stomach and nudging Joe out of the way. It read rapidly through the form and then scratched its beaky nose with one claw.

"I bet I could get them all right," it said.

"I just bet you couldn't," said Joe who'd thought of six answers to the first question alone. "Not without using magic anyway."

"Well, I won't say there aren't ways and means," the Griffin agreed, "but a creature with my brains could win easily *without* resorting to any other means."

"Cross your heart and spit on the ceiling that you'll do it without cheating?" Joe asked.

"Certainly not," the Griffin said haughtily. "I wouldn't dream of doing anything so vulgar. Now just write down what I say."

As it turned out the competition wasn't nearly as easy as the Griffin had thought it would be, but by lunchtime all the questions were answered.

"Put Mrs Chatter's name down at the bottom," the Griffin said yawning. "It'll be a nice surprise for her when she finds out she's won."

"*If* she does," said Joe.

The Griffin ignored this and went haughtily out to sleep in the back garden, quite forgetting to tell Joe about something else which had happened as a result of the afternoon they had all spent at Simmonds.

Joe went off to post his competition and then walked down to the Front to meet Grace. For some reason she had never asked him back again to her house in Lewis Crescent and, although Joe would very much have liked to have explored it again, he didn't like to press for an invitation.

They went down onto the beach by the Banjo Groyne and set up an old tin can on a stick and threw stones at it. Grace's mind didn't seem to be on the game at all for her shots went very wide, and after a while she stopped playing altogether and just sat with her chin on her knees staring out to sea.

"I don't think the poor old Griffin's ever going to find his Treasure," said Joe. "Time's nearly up and it doesn't seem to be getting any closer. It's begun talking in its sleep about it."

"Um," said Grace, staring towards the Palace Pier and the fish market and the noisy little speed boat which was buzzing importantly through the waves like an angry hornet.

"I shall miss it when it goes," Joe said. "It's been a lot of trouble, but at least it is company."

"Joe," Grace said suddenly, "I've got something I must——"

"Got it," shouted Joe as his pebble caught the tin fair and square and sent it rattling down the beach. He ran after it and set it up again and then turned back to Grace who was looking very miserable.

"Here, you can have first go this time," Joe said.

"I don't want to play," Grace said.

"What's the matter? Got tar on your dress or something?"

Grace shook her head.

"I was going to say, that is . . ." she began.

"Get on with it," Joe said. "You look as if you'd lost sixpence and found a penny, not that *that* would worry you of course," and he laughed at the thought of Grace with her million pounds missing even a hundred sixpences.

"Oh, shut up," Grace said furiously. "I wish I'd never met you."

"Now look here," said Joe getting angry too. "What am *I* supposed to have done?"

"Nothing. It's me. Oh, never mind," shouted Grace jumping to her feet. "Anyway, I've got to go home now."

"But why?" asked Joe, who couldn't follow this odd behaviour at all.

"It doesn't matter and I don't suppose I'll be seeing you again and I do hope you find the Treasure," gabbled Grace. "And it has been fun with the Griffin and everything. You see, I thought I could tell you, but I can't. So that's that."

"Grace," called Joe, but she had already gone skipping and sliding over the pebbly beach as though she was afraid something was after her.

"Girls," said Joe, and kicked the tin can right over a nearby boat because he was so angry. He went off muttering, with his hands stuck in his pockets, and made his way up the stone steps to the Top Parade and so back to Mulliner Terrace.

"Oh, Joe," said Mrs Chatter, who was waiting for him, "I can't find Tiger anywhere and he hasn't been home all night. *You* haven't seen him, have you?"

But Joe hadn't. He went all the way up and down the Terrace knocking on doors and asking, but nobody knew anything about the missing cat. So Joe went down to the Police Station—a brave move on his part as he might have met the mounted policeman, but the thought of Mrs Chatter's worry made him go—and reported the missing cat there and then went back to tea feeling very down in the dumps indeed.

"Aha," said the Griffin when it heard the news that evening, "You're a careless lot, you humans. I'd never trust one of you with a drachma, let alone a Treasure, if I had my way. I suppose you haven't noticed that something else is missing too?"

"I don't think . . ." Joe began, and then scrambled out of bed and rushed to the window and looked out at the back garden. "Oh, crikey!" he said.

"Exactly so," the Griffin agreed. "You're precious rug's gone too. It wasn't *my* job to tell you to look after it, so it's no good blaming *me*. When I did, out of the sheer goodness of my heart, try to give you a word of warning you merely told me to be quiet."

Joe sat down on the bed and stared at the Griffin. It had the grace to stop looking so smug, and began to scratch the carpet with one claw.

"You see, cats aren't as stupid as you think," it said more gently. "It must have heard me talking to the rug and picked up a word or two of Ancient Turkish itself."

"You mean Tiger's gone off on the rug?" Joe said in astonishment.

"That's my explanation," the Griffin said. "But don't worry. He'll be all right. Cats are very good at looking after their own interests."

"Oh dear," said Joe, not taking much comfort from this. "Don't you know *where* he might have gone? After all you did talk to him quite a bit."

"That animal had only one topic of conversation," the Griffin replied. "Fish. Fish raw, fish cooked, fish, fish, FISH. It may have gone to the China Seas for all I know. I did happen to mention once or twice that it was a great place for fish."

With that the Griffin turned over and went to sleep.

In the morning, when he saw how worried Mrs Chatter was, Joe was tempted to tell her the whole truth. But he knew she would never believe him so he gave up that idea and went round to call on Grace instead, to see if she could suggest something.

"She won't thank you for coming, you know," the Griffin said as they rang the front-door bell in Lewis Crescent. Then its ears went up and its green eyes gleamed. "There it is again. A distinct whiff."

"Whiff of what——" Joe was beginning when the front door opened and a pretty woman who reminded him vaguely of someone came out smiling.

"Hallo," she said. "Can I—wait a minute! You're Joe Dixon, aren't you? And this is your dog Griff?"

She pushed her duster into her overall pocket and held out her hand.

"That's right," agreed Joe, shaking it politely and wondering who she was.

"And I'm Mrs Mulligan," she said. "If you've come looking for Grace I'm afraid you're out of luck because she's gone to stay with her Aunt in Portslade for three days. Didn't she tell you she was going?"

"No," said Joe, frowning.

"There, isn't that too bad of her," said Mrs Mulligan, shaking her head. "Well, now you are here, would you care for a glass of lemonade or a biscuit?"

"No thank you," Joe said, because with so much on his mind he didn't really feel like eating. "Could you give Grace a message please? Would you tell her that Tiger and the rug have gone off together, and if she has any idea about where they might be, I'd be grateful."

"Of course I will," Mrs Mulligan said. "Tiger and the rug—I suppose it's some sort of game?"

"That's right," agreed Joe. "Thank you very much. Good-bye."

He walked away, dragging the reluctant Griffin after him. They went down to the Front and looked over the railings.

"Three days," the Griffin said heavily. "Do you realise that only two days after that, my time's up?"

"I can't be," said Joe.

"It is, you know," the Griffin said sighing. "It'll be a black mark against me and I shall lose my stripes. After all these years too. It just doesn't bear thinking about."

"I'm ever so sorry," Joe said. "I'm afraid I haven't

been much help either. Now we've got a lost Treasure, a lost cat, a lost rug and Grace is gone as well."

"Worse things happen in the desert," the Griffin said. "And after all, a lot can still occur in five days."

"I don't even know where to start looking now," said Joe, staring at a poster which said:

*Regal-Splendide. Gala Evening.*
*Come Dancing and Dining.*
*Tickets three guineas a head.*

"Let us approach the Understanding Wilkins," the Griffin suggested.

As Joe didn't much want to go back to Simmonds, he and the Griffin walked down to the Old Steine and then turned up the narrow street where Mr Wilkins lived. He hadn't come home for his lunch yet, so Joe leant against an empty shop window and kicked his heels trying not to think of poor Tiger being chased by a lot of Chinese fishermen.

"Hallo, hallo, hallo," said Mr Wilkins, coming up behind them and looking a lot more cheerful than the last time Joe had seen him. "And how are you?"

"Very well thank——"

"I must tell you," said Mr Wilkins, beaming from ear to ear, "I've decided to stop being a Demonstrator and guess what I'm going to do instead?"

"Sail round the world," said Joe, whose mind was still on the China Seas.

"Nothing as dashing as that, I'm afraid. I'm going to open an antique shop. I had the most extraordinary and quite unmerited stroke of luck the other day, and it's quite made up my mind for me. It's what I've always wanted to do, have a shop of my own. But somehow I've always lacked the courage to take the plunge. Still, that's enough about me. Are you still treasure seeking?"

"Yes," said Joe. "But we haven't had any luck at all."

"The attics and cellars of old houses are about the best places to find treasure these days," Mr Wilkins said thoughtfully.

"That's no good," Joe said. "I mean I can't just go round to people's homes asking to be let in, can I?"

"No," Mr Wilkins agreed. "I see your point. What about the Lanes then? You sometimes get very good bargains down there. Why only last Sat——"

"The Lanes," said Joe. "I never thought of that. Gosh, thanks a lot."

"Don't go and do anything rash, will you?" Mr Wilkins said anxiously. "I mean a game's a game, but you don't want to go spending your money on something that might not be worth it."

"Oh I shan't *buy* anything," Joe said, starting to move away, and then he suddenly remembered something else and skipped back to Mr Wilkins again.

"And if you were looking for a lost cat?" he asked. "Where would you go for that?"

"A lost . . ." Mr Wilkins said blinking at this sudden change of subject. "I really don't know. How—how about the Fish Market?"

"Smashing," Joe said happily. "Thanks very much."

This time he really did go, with the Griffin at his heels,

while Mr Wilkins stared after them and tried to remember if he'd behaved as oddly when he too was Joe's age.

Meanwhile Joe and the Griffin had crossed the main road and plunged into the Lanes. This small area of Brighton, which lies between the Palace and West Piers, is a jumble of very small, narrow and old streets, some of which are less than four feet across. It is easy to get lost in them, for they wind and turn back on themselves, and after twenty minutes fast walking you may find yourself back at the very point from which you started. No traffic is allowed down them, of course, but they are always crowded with people, for the Lanes are famous all over the world for their antique shops. You can buy anything in them from a rare postage stamp to a Victorian post-card, and as everybody always fondly hopes he is going to find a bargain in those small dark windows, the Lanes are always full of eager treasure seekers.

The Griffin immediately went wild with excitement.

"Great Caesar's ghost," it muttered, putting its paws up against the first window and breathing mistily on the glass. "*This* is a bit more like it."

Joe hung about behind the creature while it slowly examined everything it could see through the window and then pushed its way into the shop. But by lunch-time although it had found several very interesting scents it hadn't got a whiff of what it really wanted.

"Never mind," the Griffin said as they trudged back to Kemp Town. "We can go back again this afternoon."

Joe, however, had other ideas, and at half-past two a very sulky Griffin was being dragged round the Fish Market.

"What horrible, beastly, disgusting smells," it grumbled.

"I rather like it," said Joe, walking round a net which had been spread out to dry. He examined several lobster pots—all empty—and had a look at some of the boats, and then decided to approach a very old man who was wearing a blue jumper with Saucy Sal stencilled on it.

"I'm looking for a cat," said Joe.

"Ah," said the old sailor, whose eyes were as blue as the sea itself, "well, you'm come to the right place, boy. We got dozens on 'em."

It was quite true, for there were no end of cats hanging about: gingers, tabbies, black and whites, and quite a few which were a mixture of every kind of colouring. Joe walked up and down the beach snapping his fingers and calling out:

"Tiger, Tiger."

Some of the cats rubbed themselves against his legs, but most of them kept at a safe distance because of the Griffin.

"I'm not staying here," it said, as a big Grey Persian humped its back and spat. "This isn't my kind of place at all. I'm going off to the Lanes."

"You can't go without me," said Joe. "The Civil Guard'll pick you up in no time. I tell you what, we'll stay here for a bit longer and then go and look for the Treasure. That's fair, isn't it?"

"One fishy cat against a Valuable Treasure. You've got no sense of value at all. Oh, all right then," grumbled the Griffin.

But by half-past five they hadn't found either Tiger or the Treasure.

"Better luck next time," said Joe. "We'll come back tomorrow."

Which is what they did, with the same result. And the next day, and the day after that, until Joe's feet hurt and the Griffin's coat grew dusty and all their high hopes got lower and lower until they had almost entirely disappeared. The Griffin began to look uglier and uglier, and for the first time since Joe had met it, it seemed to have lost all its haughtiness.

"I'm finished," it said on the evening of the fourth day, when they returned to Mulliner Terrace and limped up to Joe's bedroom. "Oh, the disgrace, the utter disgrace."

"We've still got twenty-four hours left," Joe said. "Look, I've bought you a new tin of Rosey-Pol." This was kind of Joe as it had cost him his last one-and-ninepence.

"Finished!" repeated the Griffin, refusing to be comforted. "That's what comes of people doing private deals. Campbell had the stuff, Prinny wanted it—he always was a vain man—and yet it disappeared."

"What *are* you talking about?" Joe asked, looking up from his cleaning of the Griffin's bedraggled coat.

"Supply and demand," the Griffin replied, mournfully. "It's no good, I'm past it. They need a younger Griffin for the job."

"Who was Campbell?" asked Joe, hoping to take the Griffin's mind off its troubles.

"A trader in a small way of business. He had his own

ship and used to run the blockades when there was all that trouble with France. Before your time."

"What happened to him?" asked Joe. Disappointment seemed to have made the Griffin far more talkative than usual.

"He fell off his horse and broke his neck," the Griffin snapped in something like its usual manner. "I found a mention of that in one of those dull reference books, and then I saw Prinny in the museum—I still can't think of that place without remembering all my poor old friends—but between that burial house and the Pavilion there is a gap. The stuff was made, shipped, bought and then it disappears."

"Who's Prinny?" asked Joe, rubbing hard at the Griffin's front legs.

"The Prince of Wales, of course, Prince Regent, George the Fourth. Oh, your terrible ignorance—you missed a bit there, it's still dusty," the Griffin said. "Oh, the terrible disgrace."

"Now look here," said Joe overlooking the creature's rude remarks, "I'm absolutely sure we'll find the Treasure tomorrow."

"You mean well," the Griffin said heavily, putting up its beak for Joe to polish, "but I've failed. One must face facts."

But for once in its long and adventurous life it was, as it happened, quite wrong.

# 11. *The Unexpected Treasure*

THE last day of the Treasure hunt and the last but one of Joe's summer holidays was very hot and very hazy at the same time.

"There's a storm coming I shouldn't wonder," said

Mrs Chatter. "Oh, my poor Tiger. He never could stand thunder and such."

"I'm not mad about it myself," whispered the Griffin against Joe's knee.

"It'll probably pass over," said Mr Serafin, "though I said to myself yesterday that you could see Portslade far too clearly. That's always a sign of a break in the weather. Anyway, I'm going to toddle down to the Regal-Splendide this evening to watch all the nobs going to the Gala Dance. Want to come with me, Joe?"

"Yes, I'd like to," said Joe who couldn't stand the thought of spending another two hours after supper with a sighing Griffin.

Straight after breakfast they went down to the Fish Market, and the old sailor stopped mending his net and nodded to them.

"There's a storm brewing up," he said. "You mark my words."

Joe smiled politely and looked at the flat still sea which was the colour of lead. The air was very hot and sticky, and he felt as though he was only half awake. There was no sign of Tiger, and when they explored the very last shop in the Lanes they didn't get a whiff of Treasure either.

"You see," said the Griffin with miserable satisfaction, "I'm beaten. There's only six hours left till midnight."

"A lot can still happen," Joe said bracingly. "Why don't you come with me and Mr Serafin after supper? It might be quite fun."

"I shall hardly be feeling like fun," the Griffin said mournfully. "But if it'll give you pleasure . . ."

So at half-past six the three of them set out. Mr Serafin was wearing his bright white panama hat and Joe was carrying his school raincoat because Mrs Chatter had insisted that he should.

Joe had a strange tingling feeling all the way up and down his back as though something very exciting was going to happen, but when he mentioned this to the Griffin on the bus, the creature only humped its back and said it was probably because there was thunder in the air.

There were quite a few people already standing about on the pavement outside the Regal-Splendide, but Mr Serafin managed to hump and bump his way to the front with Joe tagging on behind. Mrs Chatter had given them a bag of sausage rolls which were still warm from the oven, and they ate these and made funny remarks to each other about the people who were going into the hotel.

But all the time, while the crowds got thicker and the air grew stickier and hotter, Joe felt the excitement inside himself grow stronger and stronger. Even the Griffin seemed to sense it, for it began to make odd little growling noises in the back of its throat and its newly polished coat was all hunched up.

"Oh look," said Joe, craning round Mr Serafin's stomach. "There's the Booming Lady."

"The Booming Who?" said Mr Serafin who was using his panama like a fan.

"There," said Joe, pointing rather rudely at the large elderly woman who was just being handed out of a shining Rolls-Royce.

Joe hadn't seen her since they last met in the Super-

Market, but she wasn't the sort of person you can easily forget. She was looking very splendid this particular evening in a black dress with a long train. She had a glittering necklace and earrings that shone like fire, and even as Joe watched her, her fur cape slid to the ground.

"That's Daisy Duke," said Mr Serafin hoarsely. "She was a musical comedy actress and very famous—before your time, Joe, and before mine, come to that. I used to carry a photo of her round in my pocket when I was a lad. She lives in Lewis Crescent, you know, and—"

"There's Grace," shouted Joe.

For at that moment a small figure in a stiff white party dress had slipped out of the Rolls-Royce and was picking up the fur. Miss Duke patted Grace's head and swept into the hotel. Several people clapped and cheered and Mr Serafin waved his hat enthusiastically.

"Grace! Hi, Grace!" shouted Joe.

Grace turned round and saw him and her mouth dropped open, but before she could say anything Mrs Mulligan got out of the car too and took her arm and led her into the brightly lit entrance of the hotel.

"Well," said Joe, who was both surprised and a little hurt.

And then another car swept up, and the crowd which had been growing bigger all the time shoved forwards and Joe forgot all about Grace as he tried to keep his feet.

"Keep back there, keep back," said a voice, and Joe looked up. Over the heads of everybody else he could see the figure of a mounted policeman. Joe clutched at the Griffin's collar and bobbed down out of sight.

"There's a horse about," the Griffin said, beginning to tremble. "I can smell it. Let me get at it. Let me go!"

"God bless my soul, what's the matter with the boy?" said Mr Serafin who thought it was Joe who had spoken. "If you don't like it we can leave now."

"I'm all right," said Joe, who felt that he was probably safer in the middle of the crowd than out in the open.

"My word it's a sticky night," said Mr Serafin who was quite purple in the face. "If you don't mind, Joe, I think I'll slip away and have a little something cool to drink. Would you like to come too?"

"No thanks," said Joe, holding the Griffin as tightly as he could.

"You'll be all right on your own, won't you?" Mr Serafin said. "I mean you've got that great wolfhound of yours with you and everything. But I don't think—we'd—er—better mention to Mrs Chatter that we parted company. You know how women fuss."

"I won't say anything," promised Joe, who was only half listening anyway. Mr Serafin nodded and winked and slipped a shilling into his pocket for the bus fare home, and then the crowd shoved forward again and Mr Serafin was sucked away into its middle.

"Please, please behave," whispered Joe. "If you make a fuss now anything might happen."

"I can't help it," whined the Griffin. "It's in my nature to hate horses."

"Doesn't your doggie like the crowds then?" asked a fat woman.

"Not much," said Joe, who was scarlet in the face with

heat and anxiety. He gripped the collar harder than ever while the Griffin strained to get at the police horse.

"Keep back please," ordered the policeman as another car came up. His horse, which had in its turn scented the Griffin, rolled its eyes and skipped sideways. The crowd, which was all out to enjoy itself, cheered good-naturedly.

Joe closed his eyes and dug his heels hard into a crack in the pavement. A band started playing inside the hotel, more cars drew up, and the crowd got thicker and noisier by the minute. Joe began to feel as though he was in the middle of a nightmare, but he hung on doggedly and tried to keep the panting Griffin quiet by patting its golden coat. It was like stroking a lot of little prickles.

Then there was another burst of cheering as a very important gentleman in a red coat and with a gold chain round his neck arrived. He beamed and waved his hand and began to climb the steps into the hotel, and as he did so the crowd pushed forward and Joe was shot out into the open like a pea out of its pod. He stood blinking in the bright lights for a moment and his grasp on the Griffin's collar slackened.

"I can't help it, it's my nature," said the Griffin hoarsely, and it reared up on its hind legs and howled—no other word will do—at the police horse. The horse reared up, and the crowd, caught unawares, surged backwards and then forwards again like the sea.

"It's that boy," shouted the policeman, who was revolving round and round, but who had caught a glimpse of Joe standing all on his own on the bottom steps. "I want him."

At those words the crowd suddenly stopped being good-natured and became angry instead. Perhaps it was something to do with the hot, airless night or it may have been that they were all a little frightened by the bristling Griffin—nothing makes people nastier than being afraid—but whatever the reason they all turned on Joe and their voices were like the growling of the sea as it sucks hungrily at the shingle.

As for Joe, he had never been so scared before in all his life. He stood quite still, staring at all the angry faces, with his heart hammering. He would very much have liked to turn and run, but there wasn't anywhere to run *to*, so he doubled up his fists and backed up against the steps.

Someone raised a stick as though to hit the Griffin, and Joe shouted out:

"Don't you dare touch him, don't you dare!"

"Stop that," roared the policeman, and urged his reluctant horse forwards. The crowd parted a little to let them through, and Joe retreated to the lowest step with the Griffin snarling at his side.

"Come here," ordered the policeman who was having a difficult time of it controlling his side-stepping horse.

"No," said Joe in a trembling voice. "No I won't. You shan't hurt my Griffin."

"Hurt your what?" said the policeman who was going round in circles again.

The Griffin lunged forward with all its golden claws unsheathed and its green eyes glittering, and the horse reared up, pawing with its front hooves. The crowd drew back slightly, and Joe made a grab for the Griffin's collar. It was a hopeless situation, of course, because Joe was outnumbered by about five hundred to one, but at that moment two totally unexpected things happened.

First of all there was a sudden great flash of lightning, followed almost instantly by a crack of thunder which startled everybody nearly out of his wits, and secondly a small figure in a white dress shot out of the Regal-Splendide clutching a very sleepy cat and a tattered old rug.

"Joe," shouted Grace, almost tumbling down the steps she was running so fast, "I've got him."

"It's no good," said Joe. "Get back inside the hotel while you can. That policeman's recognised me and he's after us."

The lightning sizzled violently across the sky again. Several people screamed and then hastily pretended that they had done no such thing. The thunder roared and rumbled and some drops of rain fell flatly on the steps.

"Here you," said the policeman who had now reached the inside of the circle, and he leant forward. He was very angry indeed, and you can hardly blame him for that because he was having a very difficult time of it.

"No," said Joe again. "You shan't have him!" and he dodged backwards dragging the snarling, spitting Griffin with him.

"The rug," stuttered Grace, who didn't know quite what was going on, but who had realised that Joe and the Griffin were in terrible trouble. "Oh, Griffin, the rug."

Joe forced the angry creature's head round and pushed its beaky noise against the rug.

"I won't, I won't . . ." it said, struggling furiously.

"You must," shouted Joe. "Or the Civil Guard will get you and never let you go."

"Please, oh please," implored Grace, who was almost strangling the sleepy Tiger in her anxiety.

The Griffin wrenched itself away from Joe, reared up and howled some very insulting remark at the horse which also reared up, showing its teeth and rolling its eyes more than ever. The policeman, who was an exceptionally fine rider, just managed to keep his seat, and the crowd roared harder than ever.

"That'll teach it," snarled the Griffin, and with one swift movement it twitched open the rug. "Get on, get on," it ordered.

Grace and Joe dropped down onto their knees, and the Griffin muttered something to the rug. As it did so the lightning streaked across the sky and the thunder roared so loudly that every window rattled all along the sea front.

Every single member of the crowd shut his eyes against the glare, and as they did so the rug rose rather unsteadily into the air, then flattened out and glided off into the darkness with the Griffin soaring after it. By the time the crowd had opened its respective eyes again there was nothing to see but the empty steps which were steadily getting wetter and wetter as the rain poured down with increasing force.

The policeman wiped his sleeve across his face and patted his horse which had now quietened down considerably and was just trembling slightly.

"Where's the boy?" the policeman said.

"What boy?" said someone.

"I don't see no boy," said someone else. "Cripes, what weather for September. I'm off home, I am."

"I expect the thunder upset your horse," said a fat woman, who was very fond of animals and kept three budgerigars and two goldfish at home.

"I thought I saw . . ." the policeman said, and then stopped, because in the Police Force you either see something or you don't, and it's no good telling your Inspector that you only *thought* you saw something.

Now what the policeman thought he had seen was a small boy flying up into the air on a rug with a little girl in a party dress holding a cat. And what was even worse the dog had suddenly grown wings and flown after them. All of which was quite obviously impossible.

So the policeman shook his head, straightened up, and decided that it was a good thing he was starting his leave next Monday because he obviously needed a rest. He had meant to spend his time pottering round the garden at home, but now he decided to take his wife and family to Wales after all for a complete change of air. All this went through his mind in a flash, and when he spoke again it was in his usual firm tones.

"Move along there please, move along," he said.

The crowd needed no second bidding. The thunder and lightning had given them all a bad fright, and several of the men told their female relations and friends who were with them that a bad electrical storm can lead to all kinds of odd hallucinations.

So everybody squelched off home, and long before any of them had got there they had all decided in their own minds that the boy and his peculiar dog were something they had imagined. As no one likes to think of himself as odd or different from anybody else, they all quietly forgot about Joe and discussed the storm instead.

The few children who had been in the crowd did try and tell their parents about Joe and Grace flying off on the mat with the Griffin flapping along behind, but of course their parents, being much older and wiser, told them not to talk nonsense and that it would be a good thing when the holidays were over because they only led to over-excitement.

Meanwhile Joe, Grace, Tiger and the Griffin, who were getting very damp indeed, were sailing along the Front. Grace had her eyes tight shut, while Joe, who was more used to flying than she was, was watching the lights flash past far below like a gleaming, misty necklace. Tiger curled himself further inside Joe's mackintosh and purred loudly. He smelt very strongly of fish.

"Here we go," said the Griffin panting heavily, "and *in* we go."

It slid sideways through the dark wet sky, hung for a moment in the air, then scrambled in a rather undignified manner through an open top window. The rug went after it and Joe and Grace landed in a heap on bare, dusty boards. The rug seemed to give a little sigh and crumpled up.

"Yes, but *where* are we?" asked Joe, peering round in the dim light.

"Her house," said the Griffin, pointing with one golden claw at Grace who shut her eyes even tighter and said in a quick, high voice:

"It isn't my house. You know that."

"Why not get it off your chest?" the Griffin said almost gently. It was still panting rather hard.

"I'm not a millionaire," Grace said. "I just made that up for fun. My name's Mulligan and I only live here because my mother's the housekeeper and we've got hardly any money at all and I'm sorry. I did try to tell you before, but I couldn't."

"Whose housekeeper?" said Joe, disentangling most of what Grace had said and wanting to get to the bottom of things.

"Miss D-Dukes," said Grace, and burst into tears. Joe pushed his handkerchief, which was wet and full of sausage roll crumbs, into her lap and looked the other way.

"What an evening," the Griffin said, blowing out its cheeks, "It calls to mind the Fall of Rome. There was a boy then, I remember, who defied the mob. His name escapes me for the moment, but I must say, Joe, I never thought you had it in you. If I have to return from my quest defeated, at least I shall take with me some happy memories. I could have beaten that horse, of course, but alas, it was not the moment for a real battle. Joe, my boy——"

"Hush, oh hush," said Joe, who was rocking backwards and forwards because he was thinking so hard. "The diamond ring, the one they found in the Super-Market . . ."

"A drink of water is called for, I think," said the Griffin, making discreetly for the door.

"Oh no you don't," said Joe. He rolled over, and got there first. The Griffin looked at him with cold green eyes.

"What ring?" it said innocently.

"You stole it that first day," said Joe, "and you had it in your mouth all the time we were out shopping. No wonder you said diamonds tasted nasty."

"I had to pay my debts," the Griffin said, gazing over Joe's head. "There's a very nasty smell of fish up here," it added, to change the subject.

"That's Tiger," said Grace, who had stopped crying and now merely looked a trifle damp. "Don't you mind about me not being a millionaire? I had to pretend, you see, because you were doing such exciting things like being a burglar and talking to the Griffin."

"Oh, *I* don't mind," said Joe. "In fact, I'm really rather glad because I understand about you not paying for ice creams and bus fares and shrimping—oh, crickey! What about Mr Serafin?"

"You haven't got the hang of magic at all, have you?" asked the Griffin despairingly. "He thinks you've gone home, of course, and *your* mother," he turned to Grace, "is firmly under the impression that you're riding back on the bus now with one of the waitresses who lives at Whitehawk."

"That's all right then," said Grace cheerfully. "Didn't you think it was clever of me to find Tiger? When Mummy gave me your message I thought and thought, and then I remembered that I'd said how super the salmon sandwiches were that we'd had for tea at the Regal-Splendide, and so when we went there tonight—my Portslade Aunt's a chambermaid and we'd been invited by her to watch the Gala people—and Miss Duke gave us a lift in her car . . ." Grace took a deep breath, "I went looking round the kitchens, and there was Tiger curled up on the rug in a back pantry."

"Jolly clever," said Joe warmly. At the mention of his name, Tiger woke up, stretched, and then sprang lightly onto the window ledge and out into the night.

"He's going home," the Griffin said. "He'll have a prowl round and boast a bit to his friends and then he'll slip into the kitchen of No. 13 by way of the window—which is the entrance you'll have to use tonight, Joe—and Mrs Chatter'll find him in the morning. I must say I'm glad he's gone. If there's one thing I can't stand it's the smell of fish."

"Thank goodness we've got him back," said Joe, getting up. He looked at the rug. It had two large holes in it and was very damp and bedraggled.

"It needs a refit, poor thing," said the Griffin. "But you won't find anybody in your civilisation who'll be able to do that, I can tell you. I'd better take it back with me. Ah well."

"I'm sorry we haven't found your Treasure," said Joe, opening the attic door.

"It can't be helped," the Griffin replied bravely. "But when I think—here, hold on a tock."

"Tick," said Grace, neatly rolling up the rug.

"Tock-tick," the Griffin said softly. Its eyes were gleaming and its coat was bristling again, and it stood quite still with one paw raised. It looked much more its old handsome self, and it was quivering all over: like a dog who's just seen a rabbit, as Joe said later.

"The smell of fish is going," it whispered. "Wave the rug, O Fair One. Freshen the midnight air."

Grave waved obediently, and the next second the Griffin was racing out of the attic and along the corridor, its claws clattering on the wooden boards.

"There's nothing there," Grace called out. "Mum and I just keep all our old trunks and boxes up here."

As the Griffin didn't even bother to reply, Grace and Joe went after it. They knew where it was by the snuffling noises it was making, so they went into the last little attic which was full of the smell of dust and hotness from the water tank which gurgled against one wall.

"Here, here," snorted the Griffin which was deep in one corner.

"It's the excitement; it's gone to its head," Joe said softly, but he went over to help.

He lifted up several large cardboard boxes, and underneath he found a very old wooden box tied with heavy leather straps.

"There's nothing in there, but old bits of china that my great-grandfather Campbell collected," said Grace, who was still flapping the rug.

"Campbell?" said Joe. "But that was the name——"

"Open it, O Slave," said the Griffin, so fiercely that Joe jumped. He struggled with the heavy straps, and at last managed to get them undone, then the Griffin, unable to wait any longer, pushed itself forward and opened the lid with its strong beak. A rather musty smell floated into the air and Grace flapped harder than ever.

"It is, it is," the Griffin said, and pulled at some sacking inside the box. It came away easily because it was quite rotten, and Joe, who had put on the light, went across to the creature and looked over its shoulder. All he could see were a lot of blue and white plates and little bowls that looked like cups without handles.

"Why, it's only china," Joe said grumpily. He was wet and tired, and he was just starting to get that flat feeling you have when a party has gone on too long.

"ONLY CHINA," the Griffin said. "Ignorant Slave, this is the service which was made for Prinny himself. See, it has his picture and crest on it."

Joe picked up a plate and took it over to the light. It looked a very ugly picture to him. It was quite like the tall, plump gentleman whose portrait hung in the museum. except that he looked vaguely Chinese in this painting,

"It was the artist's idea of what a great prince should look like," the Griffin said. "It is absolutely unique. An oddity perhaps, but *what* a collector's item."

"You mean it's worth a lot of money?" Grace asked.

"Money? Oh yes, of course, a great deal," said the Griffin. "If you had only told me," it added, turning on Grace who was standing quite still with her mouth open, "that your mother's maiden name was Campbell you would have saved me a *great* deal of trouble."

"You never asked me," Grace said simply.

The Griffin passed back to the box and eyed its contents lovingly.

"There was a private deal between the Prince and Mr Campbell," it said. "Then your great-grandfather was killed in an accident. The china must have been in a private storehouse—probably he was afraid of thieves—and when it was finally discovered, some thirty years later, by your grandfather, blue and white china had gone out of fashion. The Victorians wouldn't have approved of this kind of thing at all. They were rather a stuffy lot in some ways. I suppose this china was merely put to one side. It's lucky for you, young lady, that it wasn't used in the kitchen."

"There's an awful lot of it," said Joe, who had been counting the pieces. "Who's this rather fat lady supposed to be?" He handed over a plate. The Griffin looked at it and coughed delicately.

"Some friend of the Prince's, I dare say," it said. "Oh, the wonder of it. To think I've found my dear little Treasure. I am not defeated, not that I ever really thought I would be. I am, after all, one of the Great Guards of all time. We do not fail, we do not even consider failure and what is more——"

"Hush," said Joe, whose keen ears had heard something deep down in the middle of the dark house. They all held their breath. There was a whirring noise and then there floated up to them the silvery chimes of the old grandfather clock in the empty hall. They listened until the last note died away.

"Midnight," said Joe and Grace together.

"Done it," said the Griffin. "Done it, done it, DONE IT!"

And it so far forgot its dignity as to turn a somersault right across the dusty attic floor.

# 12. *Back to School*

EVERYBODY overslept the following morning, even Mrs Chatter. Joe didn't wake up till half-past ten and somehow the whole day seemed topsy-turvey. Tiger was the only one who appeared to be the same as usual and he kept twining himself round Mrs Chatter, mewing as though he hadn't been fed for a week. Joe and Mr Serafin had an odd sort of meal which was half-breakfast and half-lunch, and just as they finished it Grace arrived.

"What shall we do?" she said.

"I've been thinking," said Joe, who understood perfectly what she meant. "We'll have to get Mr Wilkins up to Lewis Crescent. He'll know all about the china. I say—it wasn't all a dream, was it?"

"No," said Grace firmly. "You should see my party dress. It's covered in dust. Come on."

The Griffin came, too, and the three of them were lucky enough to catch Mr Wilkins on his way home for his early lunch.

"We've found our Treasure," said Joe coming straight to the point, "in an attic just like you suggested it would be. Please would you look at it for us?"

"Well I don't really . . ." began Mr Wilkins, and then he remembered how he used to feel when he was playing games and they seemed much more important than real life, so he smiled and added, "All right. But we'll have to make it quick."

"It's a sort of tea service thing," said Grace as they rode back to Lewis Crescent in the 7a. "It's got very funny pictures of the Prince Regent on it."

"That's nice," Mr Wilkins said kindly. The Griffin smiled to itself and winked one green eye at Joe.

Grace smuggled them indoors and up the stairs and into the attic, and all the time Mr Wilkins went on being polite and pretending to be very serious. That is, until he saw the wooden chest, and then he stopped talking in the middle of a sentence and his face went first white and then scarlet.

"Oh," he said, "oh, oh, oh."

"It's not very pretty, is it?" Grace said sympathetically.

"Pretty?" said Mr Wilkins in a strangled voice. "Why—it's—it's fabulous. Oh my goodness, to think of it lying here all this while. Oh, what a find, what a treasure."

"Told you so," the Griffin said complacently to Joe.

Then there were running footsteps on the stairs and Mrs Mulligan came into the attic, looking very surprised indeed to see a strange man there. Everybody began to talk at once, and very soon Mrs Mulligan's face, too, changed colour. She sat down on an old wooden chair and held tightly to Grace's hand.

"I'd no idea it was valuable," she said over and over again. "It was just my grandfather's china, a sort of joke really. Oh, Joe, I can't thank you enough for finding it. We'll have to give you a reward."

"Well, it wasn't really me that found——" Joe began, and then the Griffin nipped his arm so he shut up. Mr Wilkins and Mrs Mulligan began to talk both at once, and Miss Duke, hearing the commotion, came slowly up the stairs and had to be told the whole thing all over again.

"How absolutely splendid," she said, dropping her handbag as she clasped her hands together in excitement. "My dear Mrs Mulligan, I'm delighted for you."

Joe picked up the bag. Miss Duke patted his head, and as she started to talk again at the top of her voice, Joe edged over to the door and slipped out. Nobody noticed him going except the Griffin which slid after him.

"Quite right," it said approvingly. "You've done your bit. It's up to them now to sort out what to do for the best."

Grace caught them up as they reached the front door.

"Oh, Joe, isn't it smashing?" she said.

"Super," Joe agreed.

"Mr Wilkins is terrified of giving Miss Duke a plate or a bowl in case she drops it," Grace said giggling. "He's hovering round her all the time."

"I don't think I really should have a reward," Joe said. "I mean it's not fair. It was the Griffin who found The Treasure."

"Oh, don't worry about that," the Griffin said, swishing its tail. It gave its rumbling laugh. "There's one thing you can be sure of, and that is that the Old Griffins Benevolent Fund is very well subscribed to. Now shift yourself, boy, it is time I was going."

"Oh, I'd forgotten that," Grace said. "Oh, I *am* sorry. I shall miss you dreadfully."

"Yes, I expect you will," the Griffin agreed. "But you'll have to make the best of it. You will find a trusty, honest friend in the Understanding Wilkins. You'll just have to make do with him."

Grace put her arms round the creature's neck and hugged it. It arched its back a little self-consciously, but seemed quite pleased with this show of affection.

"Get along now, do," it said, "or they'll be wondering what's happened to you."

"Goodbye, dear, dear Griffin," Grace said gently. "See you on Saturday then, Joe."

She went back into the house and shut the door. Joe and the Griffin walked slowly up to Mulliner Terrace, and Joe went up to his room and got the magic rug. It was still damp and it smelt strongly of Puffo and fish. Just as they were coming down the stairs there was a ring at the front-door bell, so Joe went to open it. A man in a white apron was standing on the step.

"Name of Chatter?" he asked, looking at a notebook.

"Well, not exactly," Joe said, "but she does live here."

"Fair enough," the man said cheerfully. "Here's her Superslic."

"Her what?" gasped Joe.

"Washing machine," the man said. "All right, Charlie, this is the place."

He went out into the road to a big lorry which was parked in front of the house. It had SIMMONDS written on the side in large letters.

"You mean she really *has* won a washing machine?" Joe asked.

"Naturally," the Griffin replied. "I told you she would. Now do get a move on. I'm sixteen hours overdue already and I don't want to blot my writing tablet."

"Mr Serafin," Joe called up the stairs, "there's a surprise here for Mrs Chatter. Could you deal with it, please? I've got to take the dog for a walk."

Mr Serafin came puffing down the stairs, and when he saw the lorry and the two men struggling at the back of it with the washing machine, his eyes bulged so that he looked exactly like a goldfish.

"Snakes alive," Mr Serafin said. "Well, here's a turn up for the book. Mrs Chatter's out shopping at the moment so we'll try and get that monster in place before she gets back. Well, I never did! Here, you're doing that all wrong. Let me show you how before you drop it."

He skipped nimbly down the steps and went to give a hand. Joe and the Griffin walked off quickly in the other direction, making for Whitehawk.

All the adventures and the excitement were over. Soon there would be no more Griffin and no more magic, and Joe was surprised to find that he was going to miss both of them very much indeed.

"Raise your spirits," the Griffin said, as they climbed the chalky path which lead to the Golf Club. "I never could abide people feeling sorry for themselves."

Joe thought about the way the Griffin had been carrying on for the last week or so and couldn't help smiling.

"That's better," the creature said encouragingly. "Naturally life will not be the same without me. But as I have often remarked before, I am not ungrateful for the little help you have been able to give me in your own small way."

"Well, I like that," Joe said indignantly, thinking of his brushes with the police and the long hours of searching in the Lanes, not to mention the trouble with Tiger and the stealing of Miss Duke's diamond ring.

"I thought you would," the Griffin said graciously. "I must say I didn't think much of you to start with, but you improved on acquaintance. I dare say that having me as your guide and mentor had a lot to do with *that.*"

Joe counted up to ten very slowly and by the time he had finished they were up on the chalky Downs with only the skylarks for company.

"It's most satisfactory," the Griffin mused, "to be able to return and to draw a neat line through my ledger. It's not one of the Great Treasures you know, but I dare say it will cause quite a little stir."

(He was right there. It did. There were articles about the china in all the local newspapers, and photographs of Grace and her mother and the attic with a large X over the corner where the china was found. Mr Wilkins did very well out of it too, because quite a number of people went to his shop the moment it was opened in the hope that they too would find undiscovered treasures. And some time after *that* Mr Wilkins asked Mrs Mulligan to marry him, which she did, and he never again had to live on boiled eggs and burnt toast, because she was an excellent cook although not quite as good as Mrs Chatter. However, all this was far into the future.)

"So now everything's all right," Joe said heavily.

The Griffin scratched behind its ear and looked at him thoughtfully.

"You will get a reward," it said.

"Oh yes?" said Joe without much interest as getting a reward for finding the Treasure didn't seem very important to him. He kicked at the springy turf with one foot.

"Having a few drachmas to hide away under the floorboards isn't everything," the Griffin said pompously.

"When you're grown-up you may unfortunately think it is, but we won't go into that now. However, I am arranging a suitable reward for you now."

"Thank you," Joe said politely, although he hadn't the faintest idea what it was talking about.

"It has certainly been a very educational visit," the Griffin said, looking up at the soft blue summer sky, "though personally I prefer the old world to the new. Give me the rug, dear boy."

Joe rolled it up, and the Griffin tucked it neatly between its claws.

"Good luck and good fortune go with you," it said.

"Look here," Joe said quickly. "About this magic business—did it really all happen?"

"It happened all right," the Griffin replied, unfurling its golden wings. "There's plenty of magic about if you keep your eyes open for it. Now you've got a taste for it you'll probably spot the odd charm, or spell or something, all over the place. Only do, for goodness sake, be careful. It's quite strong, some of it. Well, farewell then. You're not a bad sort really. Don't forget me too soon."

"I couldn't," Joe said truthfully.

"No, that's true," the Griffin agreed. It gave Joe a last look with its bright green eyes, ran a few steps and launched itself into the air. It circled round him twice, then soared upwards like some great golden bird until it was only a speck in the sky. Then that was gone too, and Joe was all alone.

He walked home very slowly, kicking at the curb and wondering how he was going to explain to Mrs Chatter about the Griffin vanishing. He would just have to tell her that it had run away and never come back, as an ordinary dog might have done. He began to feel lower and lower in his mind. His magic world was gone, and the old, familiar world seemed very dull by comparison.

He turned the corner of Mulliner Terrace and walked along to No. 13 with his head down, which was why he didn't see the figure standing on the doorstep watching him.

"Hallo, Joe," said a familiar voice.

Joe stopped dead and hung onto the railings for a moment.

"Hallo, Dad," he said huskily.

"I thought I'd give you a surprise," said Staff-Sergeant Dixon.

"You have," said Joe.

"It's only a short leave, mind," his father said, "because I'm leaving the army altogether just before Christmas. What do you think of that, eh?"

"Marvellous," shouted Joe, grinning from ear to ear.

"That's good then," his father said, and he smiled too. "I've been thinking for a long time that I ought to settle down a bit more. What I'd really like to do would be to open a little electrical repair shop, or something of that kind. Still, we needn't get that all sorted out now, on the doorstep. Do you think Mrs Chatter'll be able to put me up for a few nights?"

"I'm sure she will," Joe said.

He felt wonderful. It was like flying, but without a

magic rug and somehow better. He rattled up the front steps and opened the door, and his father ruffled up his hair and said:

"My word, you've grown a lot, Joe. What's been happening while I've been away?"

"Oh, this and that," Joe said. "Gosh, what a smashing reward. I understand what it meant now."

"What *what* meant?" asked his father, picking up his kitbag.

"Oh—nothing really," Joe replied.

He glanced up at the sky, and just for a moment he thought he saw a golden speck wheeling far up against the clouds above the Eye Hospital. Joe waved to it and then rushed indoors pulling his father after him.

"Mrs Chatter! Mr Serafin!" shouted Joe. "Look who's come home."

The following morning Joe, wearing his school cap and blazer, sat on the top deck of the 7a bus. He was turning over in his mind a few of the things he could have told the boys in his form about what *he'd* done in the holidays. There was quite a lot he could tell his Geography master too about places like Atlantis and earthquakes and slave uprisings, but perhaps it would be wiser to keep his mouth shut. After all, the fact that his father had come home was the best and biggest piece of news of all.

"Any more fares, please?" said the conductor, coming up onto the top deck.

"There's only me," said Joe, "and I've got my new season."

"Hallo, Joe," said the conductor. "Holidays finished are they? Well, did you have a good time?"

Joe thought things over.

"Not bad," he said.

STAY ON

---

**INVESTIGATING UFOs** 25p

**Larry Kettelkamp**

0 426 10006 9 **A Target Mystery**

The full, dramatic story of unidentified flying objects or "Flying Saucers" as they are commonly called. Visitors from other planets? Optical illusions? Or practical jokes? With the help of INVESTIGATING UFOs you can decide for yourself and even join one of the 20 or more UFO clubs in the United Kingdom. *Fully illustrated with photographs and drawings.*

**THE POND ON MY WINDOW-SILL** 30p

**Christopher Reynolds**

0 426 10057 3

The companion volume to SMALL CREATURES IN MY BACK GARDEN. The author tells you how to establish an indoor aquarium with snails, tadpoles, water-beetles and other tiny creatures easily obtainable from nearby pond or stream. A fascinating and instructive hobby for all ages. *Illustrated.*

**SMALL CREATURES IN MY BACK GARDEN** 25p

**Christopher Reynolds**

0 426 10049 2

Have you a back garden or even a yard or some-such place that you can visit regularly? There are many tiny creatures that you are likely to find there besides the more familiar snails, ants and worms. . . . And with the simplest equipment, mostly home-made, the author shows you how to create new worlds of interest and delight. *Illustrated.*

**FISHING** 25p

**J. H. Elliott**

0 426 10145 6

Fishing, or angling, is the most popular outdoor hobby for all ages. This book advises on the choice of equipment; baits; fishes, and how to catch them; do's and don'ts; and how to enjoy your angling. For the beginner and partially experienced alike. *Illustrated.*

**PETER PIPPIN'S SECOND BOOK OF PUZZLES** 25p

0 426 10102 2

Thousands of young people all over the country tackle Peter Pippin's puzzles every week in their local paper. Here is another collection to baffle and entertain the whole family!

**HELEN KELLER'S TEACHER** 25p

**Mickie Davidson**

0 426 10030 1

Helen Keller was stricken blind and deaf, and because she was only eighteen months, dumb as well. This is the life-story of her teacher, Annie Sullivan, herself part-blind, who brought life and hope to young Helen, later to achieve international fame. A story of rare courage and devotion. *Illustrated.*

**DOCTOR WHO** 25p

**David Whitaker**

(based on the famous BBC television series)

0 426 10110 3 **A Target Adventure**

DOCTOR WHO's first exciting adventure with the Daleks! Ian Chesterton and Barbara Wright travel with the mysterious DOCTOR WHO, and his grand-daughter Susan, to the planet of Skaro in the space-time machine, *Tardis*. There they strive to save the peace-loving Thals from the evil intentions of the hideous Daleks. Can they succeed? And what is more important, will they ever again see their native Earth? *Illustrated.*

**DOCTOR WHO AND THE ZARBI** 25p

**Bill Strutton**

0 426 10129 4 **A Target Adventure**

DOCTOR WHO lands his space-time machine *Tardis* on the cold, craggy planet of Vortis. The Doctor and his companions, Ian and Vicki, are soon captured by the Zarbi, huge ant-like creatures with metallic bodies and pincer claws; meanwhile Barbara falls into the hands of the friendly Menoptera who have come to rid Vortis of the malevolent power of the Zarbi. . . . *Illustrated.*

**DOCTOR WHO AND THE AUTON INVASION**

**Terrance Dicks**

ISBN 0 426 10313 0 **A Target Adventure**

DOCTOR WHO, Liz Shaw, and the Brigadier grapple with the nightmarish invasion of the Autons—living, giant-sized, plastic-modelled 'humans' with no hair and sightless eyes!; waxwork replicas and tailors' dummies whose murderous behaviour is directed by the 'Nestene Consciousness', a malignant, squid-like monster! *Illustrated.*

**THE LONER** 25p

**Ester Wier**

0 426 10022 0 **A Target Adventure**

"You haven't got it, boy. You've proved that. I think you picked the wrong name. You'll never make a shepherd". But David, a stray, or 'loner', who had chosen his name at random from Boss's Bible, proves her wrong in a breathtaking encounter with a huge, grizzly bear. . . . *Illustrated.*

**ICE KING** 25p

The story of a polar bear

**Ernestine N. Byrd**

0 426 10065 4

'Atu's stare grew more and more insolent . . . Komi's uncle grabbed his gun and shouted, "It's the man-killer! Shoot him! Shoot him!" Atu, the polar bear, whirled as Komi screamed "No! No!", and stepped forward slowly, deliberately, ready to kill or be killed . . .' A moving and dramatic story of the frozen north for all animal lovers. *Illustrated.*

**TRAVELLING MAGIC** 25p

**Elisabeth Beresford**

0 426 10161 8 **A Target Adventure**

Kate and Marcus Dawson, on holiday at a boarding-house in Wandle Heights, think Mr. Trevellick a little odd both in appearance and behaviour. He soon reveals himself to them as an apprentice magician from the sixth century A.D. Kate and Marcus then become involved with the magician in a series of extraordinary, sometimes beautiful, sometimes rather frightening adventures. *Illustrated.*

If you enjoyed this book and would like to have information sent you about other TARGET titles, write to the address below.

*You will also receive:*

**A FREE TARGET BADGE!**

Based on the TARGET BOOKS symbol—see front cover of this book—this attractive three-colour badge, pinned to your blazer-lapel, or jumper, will excite the interest and comment of all your friends!

*and you will be further entitled to:*

**FREE ENTRY INTO THE TARGET DRAW!**

All you have to do is cut off the coupon beneath, write on it your name and address *in block capitals*, and pin it to your letter. You will be advised of your lucky draw number. Twice a year, in June and December, numbers will be drawn 'from the hat' and the winner will receive a complete year's set of TARGET books.

Write to: TARGET BOOKS,
Universal-Tandem Publishing Co.,
14 Gloucester Road,
London SW7 4RD

———————————— cut here ————————————

Full name............................................................

Address..............................................................

.......................................................................

..............................County....................................

Age.............................